One Order to Go

Also by Mel Glenn

Class Dismissed!
High School Poems

One Order to Go

by MEL GLENN

Clarion Books
TICKNOR & FIELDS: A HOUGHTON MIFFLIN COMPANY
New York

Clarion Books
Ticknor & Fields, a Houghton Mifflin Company
Copyright © 1984 by Mel Glenn

Printed in the U.S.A.

Library of Congress Cataloging in Publication Data
Glenn, Mel.
One order to go.
Summary: Richie's long-standing dispute with his
father over his future plans is reaching a crisis point
until the wacky ideas of the new girl in his senior
class help him take action on his problem.
[1. Fathers and sons — Fiction]   I. Title.
PZ7.G485On   1984   [Fic]   84-5018
ISBN 0-89919-257-2

P   10   9   8   7   6   5   4   3   2   1

For Elyse,
Jonathan,
and
Andrew

One Order to Go

Chapter 1

I GET TO MY homeroom just as the late bell rings. It's the first day of my senior year. I squeeze into an empty seat next to my friend Eric, who says, "Hi," and resumes reading his usual *Soldier of Fortune* magazine.

My legs stick out into the aisle a bit, and someone who has entered the room after me almost trips over them. A few of the other kids in the row laugh. I automatically look toward the teacher's desk up front, but no one is there.

Pulling my feet in, I lean over and tap Eric on the shoulder. "Hey, Edelstein," I say. "What's up? You still planning the great revolution? How was your trip?"

"Sssh," he says, not looking at me. "I'm almost finished with this neat article on surplus howitzers."

I look around the room and suddenly feel depressed. The walls are still the same nauseous green that has haunted me for the past three years. Don't they ever paint around here?

Eric tears a page out of his magazine. "Gonna send away for a free booklet on automatic weapons. What did you say, Richie?"

"How was your trip?" I ask again.

"How great can forced detention with grandparents be?" he says, shrugging his shoulders.

"Even if they live in California?" I ask.

"No big deal, man. I told them I wanted to visit Edwards Air Force Base, but they insisted on taking me to Disneyland instead. They still think I'm ten years old." He begins to fill out the form for the free booklet.

"I think my father stopped counting my birthdays when I was seven," I say. "He still calls me 'the kid.'" A picture of my father, large and menacing, suddenly looms in my mind.

My stomach, which has been upset all morning, knots up again. I hold my stomach, take a deep breath and wait for the pain to subside, which it does.

I feel nervous today, I think, because of what I have to say, what I promised myself I *will* say to my father about the Unmentionable Subject.

Eric brushes a strand of hair out of his eyes. "Grandparents are worse than parents," he says. "They hover over you like helicopters. They don't let you breathe, man." He sees me holding my stomach. "You okay, man?" he asks. "You look a little green."

"Just trying to blend into the surroundings," I joke.

"You blend in?" he counters. "That's impossible. You're over six feet tall."

No teacher has come into the room yet, so kids are walking all around. Someone turns on a portable radio and a few guys in the corner keep time by banging on their desks. The radio is so large you need a shoulder strap to carry it.

"Actually, California wasn't too bad," Eric continues above the noise. "The girls there are so outrageous, though I could never shake my grandparents long enough to snag one. Next time . . ." He leaves the sentence unfinished, but smiles wickedly. "All they say about California girls is true, Richie. Take my word for it."

"You wouldn't know what to do with one if she fell in your lap," I say.

"Oh yeah? Just watch me," he says, "and take notes. You're good at taking notes. Maybe I'll let you write my biography one day."

"Yeah, I can just see the title," I say. "*The Mercenary Lover* — dodging bullets, breaking hearts, a life on the run."

"Go stuff yourself," Eric says with a smile. "I gotta finish filling out this form."

As he writes I think, What do I know about girls? *Nada.* Girls always make me nervous. They're always laughing and giggling, always staying together in groups so you can never get near one of them.

"Hey, Richie, how do you spell *catalog* — is it with the *ue*?"

"Either way," I say.

Eric looks around the room, puts down his pencil and says, "Richie, my man, there's a whole country out there filled with girls, real girls, not the dogs they have around here. This place is a kennel."

I look around the room. "They're not all that bad," I say. There's a real cute one over on the other side of the room, but of course she's surrounded by a lot of guys. I stare at her for a second.

"Man, that's all you do, just look," Eric says, hitting me over the head with his magazine. "When are you going to shape up and make your move? Appearance-wise, you're passable, too tall, but passable. But you need some work if you're going to make it with the ladies. Your legs are too long; you look like a windmill. You need some meat on your bones. Why don't you use my weights?"

Eric always teases me about my height. I'm sort of used to it by now. "How's working out on your weights gonna make my legs shorter?" I answer back.

"Your arms are also too long," he says.

"I'll make a note of that," I laugh. "Besides, I don't have time for girls."

"Oh, don't give me that crap," Eric says with some heat. "There's always time for girls. Only I know the real problem. Classy chicks wouldn't be caught dead walking into that luncheonette your father owns. They'd be afraid of food poisoning. You've been deprived, man. Tell your father to let go of that rope around your neck once in a while. What did you do all summer, work in the store and watch stupid reruns on TV?"

Eric has hit a nerve. The crack about my father is true, but it galls me to have Eric bring it up.

I did watch a lot of TV in the store over the summer while I cleaned the counter and served greasy meals. And I had to listen to my father tell the same boring stories to the customers all day long. My father talks all right, but he rarely listens to me.

I must make him listen to me today. I can't take his constant yelling, his criticism, his orders. Nothing but orders, day and night.

Now he's on my back about college, saying I must do better in school this year because colleges really look at senior grades. He has even sent away for catalogues and stuff. Unreal.

The truth of it is I don't want to finish high school even, let alone go to college.

Today I tell him that he's got to lay off me and stop trying to run my life. I'm seventeen and I know what I want. I want to stand on my own two feet without his feet stepping all over me.

I know my father. I just can't go waltzing into the store and say, "Hi, Dad, I'm dropping out." Not if I want to go on living.

But I have a plan this time, a good one. I'll make him listen.

"You can't spend your life watching TV, my man," Eric says. "Richie, you alive?"

"Huh?"

"Richie, what are you going to be, some professional TV watcher? Your eyes will fall out of your head."

Eric is beginning to sound a bit like my father. "I suppose you know exactly what you're going to do," I shoot back.

"Sure," he says easily. "I'm gonna be a mercenary. I told you that." He takes his finger and sprays the air with imaginary machine-gun fire.

He has told me that many times, but I have trouble picturing Eric taking over some rain-soaked African country. "You serious about that?" I ask.

"You bet. Richie, you have to have a plan for your life. You can't let things just happen to you."

"I do have a plan," I start to say, thinking maybe I'll try it out on Eric, but we get drowned out by the guy with the radio, who turns it on full volume.

"Hey, that's a neat radio," Eric says to him. "Can you get shortwave on it?" Eric and the guy start talking electronics, and Eric tells the radio owner about certain transmitters that can broadcast thousands of miles.

Still no teacher. I take out the little notebook I always carry. It's my own private thing. Sometimes I can be sitting in a class almost comatose with boredom, and a terrific idea about a story or even a poem hits me. I try to get it down on paper before I forget it.

Perhaps because the green walls still bother me, perhaps because my stomach is still sending me nervous little ripples, I start to make a list of all the places I'd like to run away to, preferably in a big white sailboat.

They're all places thousands of miles away from my father's luncheonette: China, Australia, Brazil. . . ."

"Turn off that radio!" a gravelly male voice commands.

I look up at the front of the room and see a teacher — I think it's a teacher — dressed in a baggy brown suit and horrible red tie. He has practically no hair. What he does have is wrinkled skin.

"I'm going to seat you in alphabetical order," the old man says when the radio is shut off. I notice he has bad teeth also. "Will you all stand while I read the names."

The class groans.

Eric turns to me and gives the thumbs-down sign. I know what that means. Last year, when we were juniors, we used that system to decide in thirty seconds or less whether the teacher was good, ordinary, or just dumb. With some teachers it took us ten seconds flat. When Eric's name is called he says, "Present and accounted for, sir."

I want to say something to the teacher, but think better of it. Anonymity in high school is something to be wished for. Long ago I learned that teachers pay exclusive attention to the very good and the very bad. Since I have no desire to be singled out either way, I try to make it a practice to keep my mouth shut. High school is something to be endured, nothing more than that. Perhaps Mr. Baggy-Brown Suit wishes for anonymity too, because he hasn't told us his name or written it on the board.

"Where did they dig up this guy?" Eric whispers to me.

I put away my notebook as the teacher finally gets around to handing out our program cards, which is what we've all been waiting for.

Eric gets his card, studies it for a second and looks over at me. "Same garbage," he mutters.

I look at mine and nod in agreement. It's the usual: math, English, lunch, typing, study hall, and American history. Same program every day, assembly-line education, life as a grapefruit cut into forty-minute sections.

"When do you have gym?" Eric asks softly. He really doesn't have to whisper, because the teacher, apparently exhausted from distributing program cards, is sitting at his desk doing some clerical work.

"I don't have it on my program. The computer must have messed up," I reply.

"You gotta have gym every term. It's required, state law or something," he says.

"I know that," I say. "I'll go down to the grade adviser's office after homeroom and straighten it out. We don't have any classes today."

"I'll go with you," Eric says, folding up his *Soldier of Fortune* and stuffing it in his back pocket. "They gave me American History I. I passed it last term."

"You did?"

"Don't you remember? I wrote that paper on how the North could have won the Civil War a lot sooner if the Union had better military strategy."

"Seems to me," I say, "I wrote most of that paper for you."

"Well, you're the writer," he says, smiling.

"And you're the military genius," I say, smiling back.

A few minutes later the bell rings, signaling the end of homeroom. There is a wild stampede to get out of the classroom, but Eric and I rush for the grade adviser's office, only to find a long line already there. The computer must have messed up a lot of programs. We wait together in the hallway, which is also painted green.

I lean against the wall and take out my notebook. I want to finish my list of countries.

"Writing the great American novel?" Eric asks, taking out his Swiss Army knife.

"Put that away," I say. "You'll get in trouble."

"For filing my nails? Lighten up, man." He works on a ragged cuticle. "Are you ready for this year?" he asks.

"No," I say.

"Neither am I," he says. "I just wish it was June already. I can't wait for college to begin just to get out of here."

"How come you're going to college?" I ask. "I thought you wanted to be a mercenary."

"Where better to learn ballistics than in college? Are you aware, my man, that there are over one hundred institutions in this great land that have majors in military science?" Eric announces.

"Big deal," I say.

"It is. The whole country is waking up militarily. It's about time too. They even have this place in Vermont that specializes in war games."

"I'm glad you found your purpose in life," I say.

The line to the grade adviser's office doesn't seem to

be moving. Eric continues to work on his nails and I'm up to country number 34 on my list.

"You check out any of those college bulletins over the summer, like they told us to do?" Eric asks after a few minutes of nail filing. The sound is getting on my nerves.

"No," I say. "My father has, though. I swear he's sent away for every catalogue in the continental United States. There's a shelf full of them in the store."

"I take it you're not exactly thrilled with his suggestions then," Eric says.

"Why should I be? If he's so hot about college, let him go instead of me. I'm not even sure about finishing high school," I say flat out.

"Well, you better get it together pretty quick. The way I figure it, there's only three more years before thermonuclear war breaks out." Eric has a one-track mind.

"You're weird," I say, "and will you stop that disgusting noise with your nails?"

"Who's to say what's weird anymore?" Eric says, putting his knife away. "The whole planet's gone weird. But you're not gonna catch me hangin' around here. I'm gonna rule over some island in the South Pacific. Did you know that there are some thirty islands in that region alone that are prime candidates for revolution, according to my *Soldier of Fortune*? If you want, you could be my minister of information."

"No thanks," I laugh.

"I worry about you, man. You're hopelessly adrift in the sea of life. You could try out for basketball this year — that is, if you practice."

"I got other plans," I say.

"Like what?" Eric wants to know.

But before I can answer, he is called into the grade adviser's office.

While he's inside the little cubicle, I think of the idea that has been running through my head for the last couple of months, the idea I want to discuss with my father. I'd like to be a reporter, perhaps a foreign correspondent. News programs are my favorite shows on TV. I love it when they say so and so, CBS News, Vienna, Belgrade, or Buenos Aires. I know I can't very well walk into a large city paper and say, "I'm Richie Linder, I'm here," but I want to quit school and catch on with a paper, perhaps a weekly and then work my way up to being a foreign correspondent. Another idea hits me. I take out my little notebook that I had stuffed in my back pocket and scribble down the following script:

This is Richie Linder, NBC News, live and wet from the small coastal country of Pendembu, in West Africa, where today a group of American mercenaries seized the capital city of Makeni. The leader of the coup, Cpl. Eric Edelstein, imposed a dusk-to-dawn curfew, saying in a radio address to the country, "You have to have a plan and I have many plans for my adopted nation."

College? No way. I don't even want to finish out this term. Now the trick is to convince my father of that once and for all.

Eric comes out of the office. "Everything okay?" I ask.

"Sure, man, no sweat. He just switched my history period, that's all. I think we're in the same class now. I can copy your homework."

Before I can reply, a voice from the inner office calls out, "Next." Eric calls out, "I'll wait for you" as I walk in.

The office looks like a sardine can, but with the same horrible green walls as the rest of the school. I think I can reach out and touch the walls on three sides.

"What's the problem?" the adviser asks wearily, not even bothering to look up. His bald head shines in the light of an overhead fluorescent.

"There's no gym on my program," I say.

"Let's see it," he says. He studies the card and shuffles a few papers on his desk. "I can give you gym the third period; you can eat lunch after your last class."

"Fine with me," I say.

For a second I get this wild idea about telling him I'd like to drop out.

"Well," he says, looking up, "anything else?"

He has a strange look on his face, like I'm not really there. I'm just one more program card to take care of.

"No," I say.

"Next," he says.

"Well, that was quick," Eric says as I walk out of the small office.

"Yeah, he didn't even ask me my name," I say, falling in step with Eric. We walk down the long green corridor.

"What do you care? Just so they get your name right on the diploma when you graduate."

"*If* I graduate," I say. I can just picture that diploma, green also.

"What do you mean, 'if'? Everybody graduates high school in the United States of America. It's your constitutional right."

"Look, Eric, I don't think I can take another year of this place," I say. The corridor reminds me of that last walk down Death Row. Prisons are painted green too.

"And you call *me* weird?" Eric says. "You gotta graduate."

"I don't see the point of going to school, just for a stupid diploma," I say. "School's a waste. Just a lot of tests, book reports, and compositions. Who cares?"

"Your father, that's who," Eric says.

I don't say anything. My father has promised to tear me limb from limb if I so much as breathe the words *drop out* again. In fact, last year when I got sick and tired of the whole business, cut out and hung around the shopping center for a week, he found out and practically killed me. He hit me so hard I had bruises on my arm for a week.

But that was last year. This year I have a plan.

"So how are you gonna get around your old man?" Eric asks. He has pulled out his army knife again.

"I'm telling him what I want when I get home today," I say firmly.

"Good luck, my man. And where should I bury the body?" he says, working on his nails again. "In a king-sized coffin, I might add. Your father is murder. He'd make a great military dictator."

"I'll handle it, Eric. It's my problem."

"Okay, that's cool. I'll catch you tomorrow in class, pal — that is, if you're not in intensive care by that time," Eric chortles.

"Take a walk, Eric," I say. "I want to be alone."

"You've been watching too many movies, pal. See ya."

As he leaves whistling "The Ballad of the Green Berets," his favorite song, I feel my stomach ripple again. It's time for me to go home and fight my own private war.

Chapter 2

I WALK OUT of school and head down the avenue. Clouds hang low in the sky and it looks like it might rain soon. I want to hurry and not hurry at the same time. My stomach continues to act up.

My father, I think, my own personal roadblock. What's the exact combination of words to make him see that I don't want to stay in this crappy school?

Sometimes I hate my father — no, let me change that — most times I hate him. He's a bully. All he does is boss people around. All he knows is the luncheonette and ordering me around. At times I hate him so much I want to break everything in the store. I hate him for always being there, his presence near my shoulder — he only comes up to my shoulder — like some grizzly bear. He even looks like a bear — short, fat, and growling. He spends all day in the store, like some caged animal. Only he likes it there. It's his natural habitat.

He's been worse since my mother died a couple of years ago, died of an embolism, a blood clot, suddenly, painlessly, the doctor had said. One morning, one bright sunny morning in June, she didn't wake up. At the funeral it just looked like she was sleeping late, nothing more than that. Anyway, I don't want to think about that now; it makes me feel too damn depressed. It's my father I've got to deal with right now, my crabby ogre of a father.

My mother was a nice person. Tall and graceful — I guess I got my height from her. She was always so very calm. She never shouted, never got angry. She'd always quietly but firmly stick up for me when my father got crazy. I miss her, I really do. I try not to think about her death too much, but it oozes into my mind like a small pool of water. Better not to think about it. There was no reason for her death. It just happened, that's all. But I do miss her. There's nobody on my side now.

Whenever I think about my father I get angry. I feel angry now, but if I'm gonna tell him about my plan, I gotta stay cool, relaxed, like a hunter quietly stalking his prey, or a boxer measuring his opponent. If I begin a shouting match with my father, I'll lose. No, I have to approach him quietly and firmly, like my mother used to do. I also have to speak to him when there are no customers in the store.

Right now I'm too jumpy — my stomach again. I have to calm down. I can't let him get to me like he usually does. I need some time to think rationally.

Walking down the avenue, I get a terrific idea, un-usual, but terrific. The old brown "Y" building — at least it isn't green — sits on a corner two blocks away from school. You can rent a suit there anytime and go swimming. And right now I feel like going for a swim.

Normally I'm not exactly an all-star when it comes to sports, but I'm good at swimming, always have been. My mother taught me when I was five or so. She'd take me to the "Y" and we would have a great time together laughing and splashing. When she died I went swimming a lot. I must have done hundreds of laps. It helped some.

"Haven't seen you in a long time. You've grown some," Mickey, the old pool attendant, says to me as I pay him for a locker and a suit. "Hey, shouldn't you be in school?"

"Short day today, Mickey. Is the pool empty?"

"It has water in it," he says, laughing through the spaces in his teeth."

"You know what I mean," I say, smiling.

"The pool's all yours, kid, but you've only got about twenty minutes. There's a class coming in then and you'll have to leave."

"That's okay," I say, "I just want to do a few laps."

The pool is not very big, maybe about twenty-five meters or so, but it feels nice and roomy to me. I quickly change in the locker room, open the metal door leading to the pool and dive in. There is only the water and me now, along with the sound of my stroke. Back and forth I swim, my long arms pulling the water easily, feeling my body loosening up. Even my stomach feels better.

I think, okay, Dad, here's the plan:

1. I'm old enough to make my own decisions.

2. So I've decided to quit school and find a part-time job with a local paper.

3. I'll use this year to save up some money so that next year I can move out on my own. Then I'll get a full-time job with a paper, maybe out of town.

Sounds pretty good, pretty solid, if I do say so myself. Now if he'll only go for it.

What will he say? At first, he'll say I'm stupid and start screaming. But if I keep my head, he'll see that I'm dead serious. He will have to listen to me.

I swim a few more laps until I hear Mickey shout, "Time's up, champ."

I towel off, change, and start for home. I feel much better now. I'm ready to face my burly, bearlike opponent in the ring.

My father's luncheonette sits sandwiched between two small apartment houses. He and I live in an apartment above the store. My bedroom window faces the street, and from it I can touch the big capital *L* that comes before *inder's* on one line and *uncheonette* on the other line on our outside sign. A separate entrance to the right of the store leads to our apartment upstairs, but you can also go directly to our apartment from a door inside the luncheonette that connects with the stairs.

"How was school, kid?" my father asks from behind the counter when I walk into the luncheonette.

"Fine," I say, testing the atmosphere. He seems calm — for now.

"You're home early," he says, taking a glass from the counter and dropping it into a soap-filled sink.

"Classes begin tomorrow. Today was a waste."

"School is never a waste," he growls.

Wrong move, I think. Better to talk about something else. "Isn't Ernie here?" I ask. Ernie, the counterman, works in the store in the mornings and I work there the rest of the time.

"He had to leave early," my father says. "His mother again." Ernie's mother is seventy-eight and has been sick ever since I've known him.

I grab a Coke from the fountain and sit at the counter. The store is an old one. There are twelve stools at the counter and three booths near the back. A freezer and a refrigerator occupy the back wall. There is some extra space near the back where a fourth booth was to be installed, but somehow it never got built.

I twirl on my counter stool and stare at the malted-milk machines, which remind me of giant bees with stingers. There is only one customer in the store now, Murray, a regular. He's a retired mailman or something, who's a permanent fixture around here. He actually likes my father's cooking, though he pretends not to. He also has bad breath.

"Hey, Sam, another cup of this poison," he says, tapping his coffee cup. "I gotta have something to wash down this miserable sandwich of yours."

"Coming right up," my father calls back.

Why does Murray have to be here now? Maybe he'll leave soon.

"Hey, all this gonna be yours, tall person?" Murray says, turning toward me.

"I doubt it," I answer.

"I mean later," Murray persists.

I'm in no mood for a conversation with Murray. It's my father I want to talk to.

My father comes over and pours Murray a second cup. "You eat something?" he says to me.

"I'm not hungry, Dad. I ate in school," I lie. If I took something to eat, I'd have to sit next to Murray and talk to him. I think I'd rather go hungry. Murray's dragon breath could make anybody give up food for life.

"Go upstairs and do your homework," my father commands. "I may need you later."

"But I don't have any homework," I say.

"Go upstairs anyway. I have some private business to discuss with Murray.

"But Dad, I want to talk to you," I say. Suddenly I don't care if Murray's there or not. I feel my chance and my resolve slipping away.

"It'll keep. I have to talk to Murray."

"But Dad, you can talk to him anytime. He's always here."

"Get upstairs," he says loudly. "Don't be rude to the customers."

"Yes, El Commandante," I say.

"And can the wisecracks," he says.

Beginning of round one.

Upstairs in my room I flop on my bed, flip on the TV,

and come across a rerun of "The Odd Couple." It's the one where Felix and Oscar win a new car and try to find a parking place for it. Though I know all the jokes and have seen this particular episode seven hundred times, it is still pretty funny.

At the end of "The Odd Couple" there is a special news bulletin about a man who has just crossed the Atlantic Ocean in a boat that is only nine feet long. I sit up and listen as the reporter asks the man how he feels after seventy-eight days at sea. What a dumb question, I think. The man can hardly stand up. I would like to know what the man was thinking about all that time on the ocean, what gave him the strength to go on. The water appears blue and inviting behind the two men. I would like to be on the pier with them. But a beer commercial comes on and there are no more questions and answers. Maybe there will be more details on the evening news.

I'm tired and I stretch out on my bed. I make believe I'm floating on that blue ocean.

My father calls up from below. "Richie, come down, I need you — and bring a clean apron with you."

"What time is it?"

"What do you care? You've been sleeping for an hour."

An hour? Swimming must have tired me out. "Be right down," I call. Maybe I can talk to my father now.

I walk downstairs. Unbelievable! Murray's still there. What does he do — live here?

"Take the register for a while," my father says in a gruff voice. "I've got some onions to peel."

"Dad, I . . ."

"Not now, Richie. I'm busy. Also check the register. See if we have enough singles."

My father not only owns the store, he *is* the store. The store, the store, that's all I've heard my whole life. "Dad, can we go on vacation?" "No, who will watch the store?" "Can I go to a friend's house?" "No, I need you to work this afternoon." "Can we get a new TV?" "No, I need a new freezer."

The blood-sucking store, I swear it's alive. It's a good thing I don't have any brothers or sisters or they would be galley slaves too. My horizon is not the blue ocean, but a white Formica countertop.

My father's only interest besides the store is baseball. He's a real fanatic. He quit high school to play semi-pro ball upstate. But he never got past the semipros. He was too slow, even for a catcher. Now he talks baseball all day long with the customers. He knows the lifetime batting averages of guys I've never even heard of.

As I walk over to my father, I get the quick image in my mind of a bear pawing at the ground. I hesitate for a second and decide to get a drink of water from the soda fountain. I'm not really that thirsty, just nervous.

"Dad, I . . ."

"What do you want now?" he says sharply.

"I want to talk to you." I say quickly.

"So talk."

"It's just that . . ." I stammer.

"Hey, don't leave the register alone," he interrupts.

"Do you want someone to come in and steal all the money?"

I'm caught between going back to the register and telling him what's on my mind. The words aren't coming, though. I feel tongue-tied. Talking to him about this is going to be difficult, more difficult than I thought. Last year when I brought up The Subject I saw him explode. "You quit school and I'll break your head," he had said. "What the hell do you think I'm working here for, so you can be a potato peeler all your life? You'll stay in school if I have to drag you there myself. I don't care how big you are. Without school, you're nothing, do you understand me, absolutely nothing."

That was last year.

"Well, what is it? I haven't got all day," he snaps now.

I desperately try to organize my thoughts: Senior year is a joke; grade advisers don't advise, they just sit in green rooms. I want to get out into the real world and write. I want to be that reporter interviewing that man who just sailed the Atlantic in a small boat. But it's all a jumble in my head, nothing like the plans I had formulated in the swimming pool before. Nothing is coming out of my mouth right. Later, I tell myself. I'll try later. "We're short of quarters," I say finally.

"That's the big deal? Look on the shelf under the register. You know where the change rolls are."

I retreat back to the register. At least I climbed into the ring, but I didn't throw any punches. My own father and I'm afraid to talk to him. What happened to all

23

that easy calm and firm determination? I just fizzled like a flat soda.

I feel relieved when a wave of customers descends on the store. It's like that, nothing for a while and then bingo. I'll talk to him later, I promise myself.

My father moves easily among the men who have just come into the store. "What will it be, folks?" he says lightly. I stare at the register, ring up No Sale, and put some quarters into the drawer. "No Sale," that's good. The story of my life.

My father is already talking baseball with some of the men, telling the story I've heard a hundred times before, the one about an ex-teammate of his who hit his first home run and ran to third base. "Sam," one of the men says, "did you hear the one about . . . ?"

Near the register is the pile of college catalogues my father sent for. I pick one up and leaf through it. It looks like *TV Guide* with pages and pages of short descriptions of various courses.

"Hey kid, you wanna take my money for your father's lousy sandwich?" It's Murray again, finally leaving.

"Why ain't you out with the girls, a big fella like you?" he asks. "Your father's a slave driver."

I nod in agreement.

"He should let you go out for a breather. All those pretty cheerleaders. You got a steady girl?"

"I got a million girlfriends, Murray," I say. "They're just waiting for my call." No sense in telling Murray the truth.

"Find just one, kid, and while I'm advising you like I am, don't spend your life in this dump."

My father hears that and yells at Murray, "Hey, leave the kid alone. He's got work to do."

"I bet he doesn't even pay you minimum wage," Murray says to me as he pays his check and leaves. He's right. I gotta get out and earn some money of my own. Once when I did ask for a salary my father laughed in my face.

The next couple of hours are totally insane, as more customers pack the place. My father and I work together getting orders and serving people. "One order of fries to go," he yells out to me. Time is just hamburgers, coffee, and English muffins. I help my father till closing time, and after all the customers are gone, he orders me to mop the floor.

"What am I, Cinderella?" I say, fairly exhausted.

"Just do it and cut the lip," he barks.

End of round one, my father way ahead on points.

"And hurry," he adds. "You've got school tomorrow."

Half an hour later I fall into my bed totally wiped out. I automatically turn on the TV, but I'm too tired to watch even the news. I forget about watching the reports about the man who has sailed the Atlantic.

Just before I fall asleep, I can hear my father still downstairs cleaning up. The bear walks. I don't want to be trapped in his cage, his ring. I don't, I don't. I know there is more to life than dirty dishes and customers who talk only about baseball.

My mother didn't like baseball either. I wonder if he thinks of her at all. I do, mostly at night when it's quiet. He never talks to me about her death — he never talks to me, period — he just growls. To all the customers he's perfectly pleasant; only me he treats like dirt.

Well, I'm gonna make him talk to me. And I'll hit him with my best shots, the old verbal one, two. Tomorrow, definitely, round two.

Chapter 3

WHEN THE ALARM CLOCK rings at seven the next morning I pull the covers over my head.

"Richie — get up, school," my father calls. He's already in the store. The bear never seems to sleep.

"Just a few minutes more," I shout down as I pull the covers more tightly around me.

"I said get up now! You're not pulling that routine again, not on the first day of class."

Seven o'clock in the morning and he's already giving me a headache. But I know what he's talking about. Last year I would often wake up and then fall back to sleep. It was just too much of an effort to get up, get dressed, and face those teachers so early in the morning.

"Just a few minutes more," I plead.

"Now!" he bellows from below. "Or else."

For once I would like him to say, "Good morning, how'd you sleep?" Like my mother used to do.

I dress, hurry downstairs, grab a doughnut from the counter, and am on the way out when my father grabs my arm and asks, "Did you look at any of the catalogues I left for you?"

"Yeah," I say, "sort of."

"What does 'sort of' mean?"

"Just sort of." I'm still half asleep. What's he bothering me for?

"Well, make sure you look at them good. I didn't get them for the customers. I want you to use them."

For a second I think of saying what he could do with the catalogues. Tell him about my plan now? No, that would be suicide. Not while he has my arm in a vise. Later, when there's a safe distance between us. "Yeah, yeah, I'll look at 'em," I say finally.

"Good luck," he says, releasing my arm and giving me a little jab on the shoulder.

I walk out of the door. Why wish me good luck? One day, even the first, is just like any other day. Luck has nothing to do with it. Only endurance is important, the ability to sit through endless, torturous periods waiting for the bell to ring.

On the way to school I pass by the "Y." Wouldn't it be wonderful if I could spend all day in the pool? I'd come out looking like a prune, but who cares?

I get to school and walk into my first period class, math, and take the next to the last seat in the second row. Teachers see who take the last seats and make a special note of them.

Other students begin to tumble in. Eric comes in and

sits in front of me. "Math, first period – yuck!" he says. The teacher is not there yet, so the room is quite noisy.

"You in this class?" someone across the room shouts to a guy next to me who already seems wasted for the day.

"Yeah, man," he nods, "failed it last term."

"Hey, Denise, did you get a good look at the teacher in 324? He's gorgeous," a girl up front shouts.

Denise ignores her and studies her own face in a small mirror. One boy bangs on the lockers in the back of the room. Ah yes, another delightful year. Good luck, sure.

The teacher walks in, stares at the class for a moment and announces, "Take out your program cards and make sure you're in the right room. This is Math 213. I'm Mr. Gortkin. Hey you, in the back, sit down in the chair like a normal person."

"He looks like he means business," Eric whispers.

"He looks like a football player," I answer back. Gortkin is a huge man, huge and wide. He could be drafted by the NFL.

"Let's get something straight from the beginning," Gortkin says. "This class is not a democracy." Eric gives me the thumbs-up sign. "You do the assignments, pass my tests, and we'll get along fine. I'm not interested in excuses, wise guys, or cheats. If you can't handle that, tell me now so I can drop you from the course."

"I like this guy," Eric says. "He could be a drill instructor."

It's an act, I decide. Get the offensive. I have heard this speech from hundreds of teachers, teachers who have read the manual where it says that first-day impressions are lasting ones and who assume that in the absence of teaching, order is the next best thing. It's okay by me. I certainly don't feel the need to be enlightened at eight in the morning.

Gortkin waits to see if there are any challenges to his opening words, his eyes darting around the room. There are none, so he distributes a couple of rexos outlining the work of the term and the first week's assignments. "There will be quizzes on Fridays and major tests every three weeks," he continues. "I expect you to be prepared and on time. I'm not interested in your personal problems or opinions. Just do the work and follow my orders."

Sounds familiar. He and my father must have gone to the same school together. Even if his speech is an act it's pretty impressive.

English is a little more exciting, though Eric, who got to the class before me, gives me the thumbs-down sign. I again sit near the back. Mrs. Fabrikant seems pumped up. "This is going to be a great term, I can just feel it," she says in her little girl's voice. "I know we are going to have a simply lovely time together. In our course work we will be concentrating on three classics of American literature: *Death of a Salesman, The Great Gatsby,* and *The Grapes of Wrath,* to see what they say about the American dream.

"Now I want all of us to get acquainted," Mrs. Fabrikant says, smiling at us. "I'd like to get your first impressions of the year so far while they're still fresh, how it feels to be back, and more importantly what kind of dreams you have, where you would like to go, what you would like to do after graduation, that sort of thing. I'd also like to know what you consider your strengths to be."

At least she's trying, I think. I look over at Eric, who is staring at his piece of paper, and I wonder if he's going to write that he wants to be a mercenary. I think for a second and write:

> I remember once in the third grade the teacher asked me what I wanted to be. All the other kids said the usual — firefighter, doctor, lawyer. When it was my turn I couldn't think of a thing to say. "Don't you have any idea?" the teacher persisted. I just stood there looking and feeling dumb. All the kids started to laugh. It's the only thing I can remember about the third grade.
>
> My father wanted me to play baseball. My mother wanted me to be happy. I couldn't seem to satisfy either of them.
>
> I watched a lot of TV, still do when I get the chance, which is not too often because I have to work after school in my father's store.
>
> I especially like watching the news; I can't pretend to understand all the politics, but it is really fascinating to see how the whole world, from England to Egypt, Korea to Kansas, can be brought right into your home.
>
> Maybe I can be near great people in great places. I like to write — stories, poetry, but mostly descriptions of people.
>
> My strengths? Well, I like to write, as I've said

before, and I also like to swim. My mother taught me
when I was five years old. I'm a pretty fair swimmer.

To tell you the truth, I'm not too thrilled about
school or the job I have to do after school. They're
both holding me back. But someday soon I hope to
plunge into the waters of life.

I reread the piece and quickly come to my senses.
"Waters of life"—good God, that's awful. What's wrong
with me? How can I tell all this personal stuff to a stranger
when I can't even tell this junk to my father?

But I will. I'm not gonna back down again like I did
yesterday. Get ready for round two, Dad.

I rip up the paper violently. Mrs. Fabrikant looks at
me. "I just got a new idea," I say. "That's wonderful,"
she smiles. In the remaining time I write the usual bull:
"This last year is very important because it is a stepping
stone to the future, . . ."

Mercifully, the bell rings before I have a chance to go
over this work of art.

Gym seems like a military mobilization. Mr. M. L.
Patterson reads the rules in clipped cadences, punctuating
each order with a blast on his whistle. "All right, troops,
line up," he says in a barking voice.

"Good God, you again," I say to Eric, who lines up
behind me. "I can't get rid of you."

"Luck of the draw, buddy. Neat teacher, no?" Gym
is Eric's favorite subject. I knew Patterson would get
Eric's thumbs-up seal of approval. "What's so great
about him?" I ask Eric after Patterson takes the roll,
shouts, "At ease, men," and we are just hanging around.

"It's not him so much, but what he represents," Eric says.

"What's that?"

Eric brushes away the hair that is always falling over his eyes and says, "Order, purpose, and structure."

"Running around and shooting a few baskets is structure?"

"Richie, it's obvious you don't understand the global picture. I thought you like watching the news. You're always telling me about this reporter and that one. When the next war comes, only the strong will survive. Physical fitness is very important; it's your body – you have to take it home with you. Muscle tone is everything."

"Spare me the physical fitness ad," I say. I look down at my own reasonably flat stomach. "Besides, I'm in pretty good shape – from swimming."

"Anybody can swim, even babies. You gotta put in the time on the heavy equipment. A Nautilus machine would do wonders for your biceps. The heaviest thing you lift is a bran muffin."

"Eric, why don't you go . . ."

Patterson blows his whistle just then and for the remaining time in gym we run some laps. Eric jogs over. He isn't even breathing heavy. "You got lunch now?" he asks.

"No, typing." I say.

"See you later then," Eric says, jogging off.

I can't believe my eyes when I walk into typing. There, in front of the room, is the most beautiful teacher I have ever seen in my life. This is a fox, first class. She

33

has long blond hair, green eyes, and a toothpaste-ad smile. Above and behind her on the blackboard is her name: "Ms. Poquette." She must be a flight attendant on leave from Air France.

Shimmering Ms. Poquette asks for someone to distribute some material. I think about volunteering, but before I can, about ten guys have already jumped up to help.

Let me tell you about girls. They scare me. The more beautiful they are, the more they scare me. Even ordinary ones leave me petrified. The plain fact is that I'm not all that experienced when it comes to girls, but movie stars are a whole 'nother thing, and Ms. Poquette definitely qualifies as star material.

One thing I'm proud of is that I've taught myself typing and practiced on my mother's old Remington. So for the rest of the period, while the other students are trying to get the hang of the home keys, I watch Ms. Poquette. I wonder why anyone as pretty as her would want to become a teacher, and what her first name is — probably something romantic, like Darlene, Nicole, or Danielle.

The bell rings, and with Ms. Poquette's lovely face etched for eternity into my brain, I go next to study hall, which is located in the library.

The library looks like a Gothic tomb. It is one of the few places in the school that is not painted green, but a dark, musty brown. At each table there are two or more chairs and a cute little lamp covered by a tan shade. Last year, when I was seriously into cutting classes,

I would come here and sit at my favorite table, a small one near the back, next to the reference section. It was fun to reach back, pull out an encyclopedia volume at random and begin reading. And it was a great place to write. No noise. You could hear people breathing; it was that quiet. Not that Mrs. Resnick, the librarian, doesn't let you talk – she does as long as you whisper.

I walk back to my favorite table, wave hello to Mrs. Resnick, who nods hello back, and sit down in my old seat. It feels comfortable. I take out my writing notebook, think for a second and begin:

Outline: TV news profile
Subject: Ms. Poquette – the woman and her world
Reporter: Richie Linder, ABC News

There are many paths to education, but none so glamorous as the one chosen by Ms. Danielle Poquette of room 328. Armed with a stopwatch and a smile, she brings a touch of class and a career in aviation to the local high school. "I knew being a flight attendant couldn't last forever," she says, "so I wanted to do something to help the young people of today get off the ground, so to speak. . . . "

Suddenly, a voice interrupts my daydream.
"Is this seat taken?"
I look up to see an explosion of red hair, heavily made-up eyes, a lumberjack shirt and paint-smeared jeans. It's a girl. . . . I think it's a girl, though I'm not too sure. She throws a book bag on the table. There are things hanging out of it.

"No," I say, wondering why, when there is a whole library to sit in, this girl decides to sit near me. I don't want to be bothered by any weirdo.

"You stuck here too?" she says sweetly. Her accent sounds faintly southern.

"Guess so," I say, annoyed that my Ms. Poquette idea was becoming distorted like some broken TV picture.

"I hate sitting alone," she says, taking the chair next to mine, "and you look like you need company."

"I do?" All I want to do is write. Who is this space cadet? Maybe I can change my seat.

The girl is impossibly friendly.

"I'm Lana Olivia Turner," she announces. "Don't even say it. My father loved old movies. When I was a kid he would drag me to the movies all the time. He would keep me quiet with popcorn. I swear I had a permanent stomachache for two years."

I look quickly past her. Mrs. Resnick will probably throw both of us out.

Lana catches my nervous look. "Hey, are we allowed to talk in here, or is this a Trappist monastery or something?"

"It's okay as long as you keep your voice down," I say. The girl is embarrassing me. I hope I don't see Eric; he'd never stop ribbing me.

"I can deal with that," she says in a lower voice. "Ain't this school the pits, though? I walked into the record office today and they didn't even want to know my name, just my social security number. Can you beat that? You could drop dead on the steps and nobody would know the difference." She giggles a bit at her own joke and then starts to rummage through her book bag.

"I know what you mean," I say sort of politely. "I had the same thing happen to me in the grade adviser's off——"

"I had a safety pin here somewhere," she says. "The pocket's coming off my shirt and I'd hate to lose it. It's my absolute favorite shirt. Where was I? Oh, yeah, this school's like a kindergarten, a pass for this and a pass for that. I feel like an absolute moron when I have to go to the john carrying this huge wooden pass."

I feel like I'm watching a clown on TV, a refugee from Ringling Brothers Circus. Lana catches her breath, but only for a second. I still haven't said much.

"I mean, the nut jobs they have for teachers," she rambles, "what a bunch of airheads! Last period I opened the window in my history class for some breeze, you know, and this higher form of plant life for a teacher starts screaming at me, 'Don't you know that the bottom windows have to be closed?' What did he think I was gonna do — jump? Come on, really. Say, you don't talk much, do you?"

"Not in libraries," I say.

"You saying I talk too much?" Lana says with a grin, really her best feature. The rest of her is, well, raggedy. On her hands are four rings, which catch the light from the table lamp.

"I don't talk much, remember?" I say.

She claps her hands in surprise. "Oh, a witty member

37

of the species. That's good. I like to have intelligent conversations. Are you intelligent?"

"Reasonably," I say. She is interesting; I'll say that much for her.

"You're not stoned, are you?" she says out of the blue.

"Me? No," I say, taken aback. "Are you? Are you always like this? So up, I mean."

She removes one of her rings, looks at it for a second, and then switches it to her other hand. "I'm straight. Drugs are for losers," she says. She stops talking and stares at me. Her eyes are really quite nice, if you would take away all that gop on her face.

"Something wrong with my face?" I ask after a few moments of uncomfortable silence.

"No, it's a nice face," she says lowering her eyes. "I was just making a decision. I've made it and I'm going with my feelings."

"What are you talking about?" I ask.

"I've just decided we're gonna be friends. Any objections?"

"Just like that?"

"Yep," she says, "the vibes are good. You're cute-looking too."

I feel myself blush. I don't know what to say. No one has ever called me cute, except my mother.

"Do you mind if I knit while we talk?" From her book bag she pulls out a mess of yarn and knitting needles. "I'm making a sweater for my father. His birthday's in a couple of weeks. Do you like it?" She holds up a blue sleeve.

"Yeah, it's nice," I say.

She looks closely at the sleeve. "Thanks, but it's not all that good. I'm just learning. I want to be totally self-sufficient, maybe live by myself in the woods for a couple of years, like that guy Thoreau did."

"Why would you want to do that?" I ask.

"Because civilization sucks. Witness this school. You lose touch with yourself. Ever read *Walden*?" Lana asks.

"There was a selection from it in my anthology last term," I say.

"No good. You gotta read the whole book. He really gets in tune with nature. Know what? I'm gonna get you a copy. They must have one in this library," she says, starting to get up.

"No, it really isn't . . ." I start to say, but by this time she is out of her seat on her way to the card catalogue.

I watch her go, her lumberjack shirt flapping around her hips. What a character! Maybe for a story? I pick up my pen and try to describe her, write down some impressions. She is not easily described. By now she is talking to Mrs. Resnick. Lana then walks back to me.

"Can you believe it?" she says. "One copy of the book in the whole place and someone copped it. Thoreau sure had it right about civilization." She sits down. "Sorry."

"That's okay," I say. "I can live without reading it. I always thought he was sort of running away anyway."

"What's wrong with that?" Lana says sharply. "He just didn't want to get trapped by the system."

"You can't always do what you want," I say, closing my writing notebook.

"Sure you can, sweety," Lana says quickly. "Hey, what do you do for kicks around here? Are you a basketball jock? You look tall enough."

"No," I say, trying to think of something. I don't want to tell her about my writing. "I swim sometimes. Only I don't get much of a chance to do that anymore. I work after school."

Lana picks up her knitting again. "Pity that," she says. "What do you want to do that for? You're going to be working your whole life someday. Now's the time to enjoy yourself, do what you want."

"It's not that easy," I say quietly. "I don't have a choice. I have to work."

"There are always choices," she says with finality.

That's true, I think. A picture of my father flashes through my mind. Another topic I don't want to talk about. Instead, I return to something safer. "You just move here?" I ask. "I haven't seen you around."

"Moved here last month," she says, holding up the blue sleeve to the light. "My mother insisted I finish high school under her protective eye and away from my father. My parents just got a divorce. Now they're like every other couple, fighting via long distance. Your parents divorced?"

"No," I say, and nothing else. Doesn't she keep anything private? Lana notices my writing book on the table. "What's that?" she asks.

"This? Just a notebook," I say quickly.

"For school?"

"No, just my writing book. Whenever I'm bored in

class I write a few things down," I answer somewhat hesitantly.

"Like what?" She certainly is persistent.

"Nothing much, really. I like to watch people and get them down on paper."

"Am I in there?" She makes a grab for the notebook. I pull it away.

"No," I lie, "I just met you."

"Can I see your book?" she asks sweetly.

"Er — no, it's pretty rough," I mumble.

"So you're a writer, ah-hah."

"Ah-hah, what?"

"Nothing, really," she says, putting her knitting in her bag. "Only that I was wondering about you. You're much too polite, you know that? At least on the surface. I bet there are some raging storms underneath. What are they?"

This girl is much too pushy, too nosey.

"Okay, okay, don't get so uptight," she says when I don't answer. "Listen, what time is it? I gotta go back to the record office. They want to straighten out my records. Fat chance." She picks up her book bag. "Have a good day. I'll see you tomorrow. Keep on writing and say nice things about me."

She walks quickly out of the library, her book bag banging against her hip and her long, tangled red hair bouncing against her shoulder. I watch her go.

I open my writing book to where I had scribbled some words about Lana: weird, crazy, rings, red hair, nice smile. Now I have to figure out a story for her.

I write for a few more minutes until the bell rings. When it does, I walk to my next class still trying to figure out who or what I have just met.

In history I see Eric waving at me from the back of the room. "Saved a seat for you," he says.

"What gives?" I ask as I see a fairly young man with blotchy skin and blond hair trying to bring the class to order. Eric shrugs his shoulders. Paper airplanes already dot the sky. Kids are sitting on desks and are shouting all over the place. Several girls are conducting a makeup seminar in the back. I have seen this film before — *The Blackboard Jungle*. I look at the teacher, who seems frightened, but he presses on anyway. He spends practically half the period distributing textbooks and toward the end of the period he begins to write some notes on the board. The class quiets down somewhat.

We write until the bell, and when it rings kids almost trample one another to get out. I catch up with Eric, who says, "He can't control the class, not strong enough. Either you have it or you don't. How was study hall? I thought I saw you going into the library."

"Okay, I guess. I met this weird girl, though. Her name is Lana Olivia Turner."

"The one with the bag full of strings?" Eric asks.

"You know her?" I say, surprised.

"She was in my shop class this morning. What a flake. She asked the teacher whether killing trees to make bookends damages man's relationship to God. What an oddball."

"I don't know. She said I was kind of cute," I say with a smile.

"See what I mean?" Eric says. "A definite crazy. Listen, you want to come over to my house? I want to show you this neat book I have on attack submarines."

"No, I gotta get home. My father expects me. I'm late as it is."

"I'm glad he's not my father. There'd be a war." Eric has met my father more than once. They did not exactly hit it off. "Where did you find him?" my father said, like I brought home a snake or something.

"I gotta run," I say to Eric. "See ya."

Sure enough, when I walk into the store my father looks up from the dishes and snarls, "Where the hell were you? You're late."

"Only a few minutes. I was talking to Eric. What's the matter, the store's empty." There's only one customer in the store, a well-dressed man at the end of the counter.

"Ernie had to leave again. I had to handle the lunch rush myself," my father says with annoyance.

"I'm sorry," I say.

"You come home as quick as you can, you hear?"

"Yes, sir," I say, with military precision.

"And clean off those tables. Don't they teach you anything in school about responsibility?" he growls.

"Look, I said I was sorry," I snap back.

I go get a damp cloth. Where is it written you have to love the father they give you? I mean, what choice do you have. I clear the dishes and drop them into the sink.

"One more thing," my father says fiercely. "Take

a look at those catalogues I left for you. Maybe they'll give you some ideas."

I don't say anything, but continue to wash the dishes.

"You hear me?" he says.

I still don't say anything, and that infuriates him. "You turn around when I talk to you," he says loudly.

"Stop shouting," I say. "I can hear you."

I can feel round two beginning. Okay. Let's have it out, here and now – I'm ready.

44

Chapter 4

"WHY ARE YOU pushing college on me?" I ask easily.

"Pushing college, get that will ya," he says with a forced laugh, looking up at me. "I'm giving you the chance to make something of yourself, and you make it sound like I'm stuffing medicine down your throat."

"I don't want to go to school — high school or college." There — I've said it.

"What the hell are you talking about?" he growls, his face growing redder. "Of course you're going to college." He bangs his hand on the counter for emphasis and looks down toward the end to see if that well-dressed man looks up. But the man continues to stir his coffee undisturbed by our growing argument.

"I've got other plans," I say suddenly. My father turns his head back to me. He's not going to push me around, not this time. "I've got other plans," I say again.

"You do? Like what?"

"I'm dropping out of school. I'm sick of it. I'm gonna work for a newspaper, be a journalist."

"Just like that, huh? Where do you get your crazy ideas – from TV? TV is not real life. Who's gonna hire a kid like you?"

"Lots of places."

"Sure, and I'm going to play major-league ball."

"It's something I can do," I say. So far, so good. I feel I'm holding my ground in this round.

"Who says?" he says looking straight through me. "I've seen your grades in English and they're not all that hot."

I'm ready for that one. "Dad, you can't learn to write in school."

"Where else then?"

"On the job. You learn from the ground up. There's lots of papers and TV stations across the country."

"That's crazy, really dumb. So now you're going to be a big TV star. Terrific. Who's been feeding you this crap – Eric?"

"It's my own idea," I say, my voice rising and becoming a bit squeaky. Keep your cool, I warn myself.

My father takes a dishcloth from behind the counter and wrings it out very hard. "Sounds like it," he says. "Stupidest thing I ever heard of. I've been thinking you could go into hotel management or something like that. You already know how to cook."

"I'm not interested in things like that," I say. "I'm over sixteen. I can do what I want. It's my life."

46

"So stop ruining it," my father snaps back. "I dropped out of school, and I'll be damned if I let the same thing happen to you. I don't want you winding up behind some freakin' counter like me."

"But you love this store," I point out.

"It's a lousy luncheonette, that's all. Look around, it's a dump. We all have our jobs to do. Yours is to stay in school, go on to college, and mine is to stay here. You don't know how lucky you are. Your whole life's ahead of you."

"So let me live it my own way," I declare firmly.

"And what way is that? You don't have a clue, just some cockamamie idea about writing. Who are you, Dan Rather? You might as well tell me you're going to be an astronaut. Let me guide you a bit," he says.

"Guide me? You're running my life," I say frantically.

My father lets out a sigh. "You know something, I can't tell you a thing. Nothing. But I'll say this much. As long as you're living here you'll do as I say. You better believe that."

Two customers come into the store for some cigarettes, and my father changes his tone in mid-sentence, practically. "Anything else?" he asks them. To me he snaps, "Don't you have any homework or anything?"

In fact I do — Gortkin's. Some exciting math problems. It's not enough they have to torture you in class. But I don't feel like doing homework. I want to settle this thing now.

"Dad," I say, aware of the cracking in my voice, "let's talk, I want you to hear my whole plan. I . . ."

"Hey, Mac, you want some more coffee?" my father calls out to the guy at the end of the counter. The man looks up, shakes his head no, and continues reading a newspaper.

"Dad, I . . ."

"There's nothing to talk about, Richie. Case closed." He cuts me off. "That's the trouble with kids. All they want to do is talk. God forbid they should do anything. I see the bums who come in here; you want to be a bum? Let me tell you again, kid, as long as you're living under my roof you'll do as I say, like it or not. That's final."

In my head I hear a bell signaling the end of round two. The score is two rounds for my father and none for me.

"Listen, Richie," my father says, "watch the store for a while. You've given me a migraine with all this crap. I'm going upstairs to lie down. Finish up the dishes here and see if that character on the end wants anything else. Call if you need me." He takes off his apron and trudges out of the store.

I plunge my hands into the sink full of dirty dishes. The guy at the end of the counter folds up his paper and starts walking over to me. Good, I want to be alone.

Eric wanders in just then. "King Kong around?" he asks.

"He went upstairs," I say to Eric, wiping my hands on a towel. "What do you want?" The customer with the paper suddenly turns back and motions to me for another cup of coffee. I get him his coffee and then go back to my dishes.

"I thought you might want to go over to the shopping center and check out the action," Eric says.

"The girls?" I say.

"No, the parade of camels masquerading as girls. What do you think I mean?" Eric says with exasperation.

"I gotta stay here and work," I reply. "See these hands? Full of soapsuds."

"A convenient excuse," Eric says easily.

"Big man," I say, staring at him. "I don't see you picking up winners Saturday nights." I shoot a soap bubble at him.

"Just waiting for the right one," he says taking a pretzel from a jar on the counter.

"She hasn't been invented yet, Eric. I don't know many girls who head their own commando units. And that'll be five cents for the pretzel."

"Put it on my tab," Eric quips.

"You don't have a tab."

"Start one for me, then. Hey man, what's this?" Eric says leaning over the counter and picking up one of the catalogues my father left for me.

"What do you think it looks like?" I say, annoyed. "You want it?"

"Me? No, I'm all set. Filled out my SAT application, financial aid form, even got three teachers to lie about me for recommendations—the whole bit," Eric says, a bit smugly.

"Have you decided where you're going?" I ask. Maybe Eric should be my father's son.

"Narrowed it down to two or three military schools down south. They respect tradition down there. Why don't you come with me? We could be roommates; it'll be great. We could rise through the ranks together."

"Come off it, Eric." I tell him.

"Well, don't say I didn't give you the chance. Richie, wake up. This is a high-tech society. The way I see it, computers and the military are the waves of the future. You're just not aware of what's going on." Eric can be impossible at times.

"Guess not," I say, thinking of the battle I lost with my father. My friend is going to be a military genius and I'm up to my elbows in soapsuds. When do I get on with my own life?

"Listen, pal," Eric says taking another pretzel. "I gotta split. Hold down the fort."

"Who's gonna take it?" I say as he walks out. Who would want it?

I wash some more dishes and finish up. The one customer is still drinking his coffee. Strange, he's been there a long time. There must be something magical about the store that sucks you in and keeps you stuck in it.

With nothing really to do, I pull a *TV Guide* from the rack and flip through the pages. The college catalogue Eric picked up is still on the counter, but I don't feel like looking at it.

"Excuse me," a voice says.

I look up. It's the guy who's been sitting there for years. Good. Maybe I can catch a movie on the TV we have in the store.

"What do I owe you for a tuna fish sandwich and a cup of coffee," he says. "Make that three cups."

"Two forty," I say impatiently. I want him to leave so I can watch TV in peace.

The man looks quickly around the store.

"Be a good kid and let me have all the money in the register," he says.

"What the — " I stammer.

"Just do as I say and you won't get hurt, big fella." His voice is very gentle.

I didn't see this movie. He steps closer to me.

"My father will hear you, he's got a gun," I bluff. My head is beginning to spin; I feel dizzy.

"Bigger than this one?" the man says, pulling out something black from his pocket. A gun? A knife? I don't know. My head is whirling. I feel frozen. He's gonna shoot me! (Film at eleven) I can't seem to open the cash drawer.

"Quickly kid, if you want to see your next birthday," he says.

"Yes, sir," I say.

I manage to get the register open and give him all the money. My hands are shaking.

"Thank you," he says. "And have a pleasant day."

I stand there shaking. It's a few seconds before I can get myself to move. Then I run upstairs screaming, "Dad! Dad!"

He's in the bathroom. I hear the toilet flush.

"Dad, Dad, come out!" I scream, banging heavily on the door

"What are you doing here?" he says through the door. "Are you crazy, leaving the store alone?"

"Dad, please!"

He opens up the door and sees the wild look on my face. "What's going – " he starts to ask.

"We got held up!" I blurt out. That guy, that guy at the end of the counter, I think he had a gun, he was gonna shoot me. He made me – "

My father pushes me aside and runs down the stairs faster than I've ever seen him run before. I follow him. He goes straight to the register, looks inside the cash drawer and slams it shut in disgust. "You gave him all the money?" he says turning on me.

"He had a gun, Dad," I remind him.

"That's what you say. Did you see it? Did you see a gun? What did you do, stand by and let him walk right over to the register and help himself?" he snarls.

I don't believe this! He's blaming me!

"It wasn't my fault," I say, close to tears. "I swear it, he had a gun. I'm sure it was a gun. It wasn't my fault."

"Of course it was," my father says through clenched teeth. "A guy spooks you with I don't know what, probably his finger, and you let him clean me out. Sure it's your fault. If you hadn't started in on me with your stupid ideas about quitting school, none of this would have happened. If you hadn't given me a giant pain, I wouldn't have had to go upstairs. He was just sitting in

52

the store waiting for the right moment and you gave it to him."

I start to cry. I can't help myself.

"What the hell are you crying about?" my father yells. "Go upstairs. I'm gonna call the cops. I don't want them to see I've got a crybaby for a son. I can't stand to look at you. Get upstairs."

He gives me a look of utter contempt, like I'm worse than a bug. "Get!" he bellows.

I run upstairs, turn on the TV and throw myself on my bed. My fault? The guy had a gun, didn't he? Maybe it was my fault. Maybe I could have done something, I don't know. I try to replay the robbery scene in my mind, but it all happened so quickly, like fast-forward on a projector. Did he have a gun? I think so, but I don't know really.

What hurts the most is that look on my father's face, a look that said: You're no son of mine, you're worthless.

It's not the first time I've seen that look.

Crazily, I remember the first baseball game my father ever took me to. I was only seven, but even then I thought that I was at the game just to please my father. I really wanted to watch Errol Flynn as Robin Hood on the afternoon movie, but my father decided that it was to be the day I would be introduced to the wonderful world of professional baseball.

I looked at the people in the stands. They were more interesting than the players on the field.

"Watch this guy pitch," my father said. "He has a wicked curve ball."

I hardly knew what a curve ball was. I saw another kid with some cotton candy.

"Daddy, can I have some cotton candy?" I asked.

"Not now."

"Please," I pleaded.

"Later. You're missing all the action — men on first and third."

"But I'm hungry," I said.

"You ate at home. Sit still and watch," he said more firmly.

"Please?" I begged.

My father finally gave in because he wanted to watch the game. The cotton candy tasted nice and gooey. "Daddy, how do they make baseballs? My friend says there's a string inside. How can there be string inside?" I wanted to know.

"Not now, Richie, can't you see we've got a rally going?"

What's a rally? I pulled at the spider web of candy and looked out over the field at the scoreboard. I liked the way the lights flashed on, like a TV screen with yellow numbers.

"Dad, I have to go to the bathroom," I said.

"Now?" he asked in annoyance.

"I have to go."

"Shit," my father said.

My father took me. As we came out of the bathroom that was tucked behind the stands, there was a loud roar from the field. "What happened? What happened?"

my father asked somebody nearby. He was pulling my arm, dragging me.

"Home run! Home run! Didn't you see it?" the fan said.

"I was in the bathroom. I didn't see nothin'," my father said. He turned on me. There was a wild look in his eyes. "Remind me never to take you to a baseball game again. You spoil everything."

I burst into tears. Errol Flynn would never have said that.

I don't remember anything else about the game. All I can think of is that horrible look in my father's eyes.

It is as clear now as it was then. My father wants a different son, one who enjoys baseball, gets good grades, goes cheerfully to college, and can handle customers and even robbers in the store.

He wants too much. And I know for certain he doesn't want me.

I hate him, hate him. And I hate my mother also for leaving me with this monster.

I turn toward the TV. The weather man is saying something stupid about how he can't do the sports report. There are no more bulletins about the man who sailed the Atlantic in his small boat.

"Hi, kiddo, how ya doin'?"

It's Lana the next day in study hall in the library. "I didn't know you could draw," she says picking up the piece of paper I had been doodling on. "What do we have here, boats of every size and description," she says cheerfully. "Hmm, very interesting. Freud would say you have a deep desire to relive the embryonic experience."

"Give me that," I say grabbing the paper and looking at her. I hardly recognize her. She is dressed in a yellow camp shirt, a denim skirt, a brown sports jacket, and blue and yellow Nike running shoes. Actually, she looks quite good — annoying, but good.

"Hardly a friendly greeting," she says. "Try saying hello."

"Hi," I say. The truth is I don't want to speak to anyone, especially after last night. I was a robot in all my classes this morning, not speaking to anyone, not even Eric.

"'Hi.' Is that all you can say? Listen, you may be cute, but you do have to hold up your end of the conversation. Ask me why I look like a model today," Lana says twirling around.

"Why do you look like a model?" I say dully.

"Thought you'd never ask," she says, smiling. "My mother hid my jeans, threatened to burn them. Can you beat that? She actually expects me to wear dresses, for cryin' out loud. How gauche." Lana sits down next to me. I think she even has some perfume on. "By the way, Smiley, do you have a name or what?"

"Richie," I say.

"Wonderful, it talks," she says clapping her hands in mock glee. "We're on the way. Look, pal, I'm making a conscientious effort to be bright and cheerful, but you're not helping. My new shrink says I've got to reach out to people. Makes me feel like a telephone commercial. Why so down?"

"It's nothing. I don't want to talk about it," I say.

"You want the number of my shrink?" she says playfully, poking me on the shoulder. Then she takes out her knitting.

"Just leave me alone," I say.

She doesn't. "Oh, come on," she says, "what's the problem? No date for the prom? Come on, give. Catharsis is beneficial for the soul."

She won't leave me alone. Why doesn't she go bother someone else? There are a few kids near the card catalogue she could annoy.

"I'm all ears, Richie. Unburden your heart," she continues brightly.

"I got held up last night," I blurt out. Anything to stop her damned cheerfulness.

"What?" she says, her face suddenly turning serious.

"My father's store, a luncheonette," I explain.

"What happened?" she asks with concern.

"I just told you," I say.

"I mean the whole story," she says.

"Not much to tell," I say. "I was at the register and all of a sudden this guy comes up to me and demands I give him all the money in the drawer." I leave out the part about the gun; I'm too ashamed to mention it.

"What did you do?" she asks.

"What could I do? I gave him all the money and he left," I say flatly.

"Wasn't there anyone else in the store, your father or something?"

"He was upstairs," I explain.

"What did he say?" Lana's questions are making me feel like I'm on a witness stand.

"What did he say?" she persists.

"About what?" I ask.

"About the gross national product, brain. About the robbery, of course," Lana says excitedly. What is she getting all worked up for? I'm the one who got robbed. I can see Mrs. Resnick, the librarian, looking over our way. I put my fingers on my lips. "He started shouting at me," I whisper, "like it was my fault or something, asking how much money the guy took and all."

"I guess your father called the police," she says.

"Sure. They were just great. They looked bored by the whole thing."

"Well, it's routine for them," she comments.

"Well, it wasn't routine for me. I'm still upset."

"I can see that," Lana says. But she doesn't say anything more, and continues with her knitting. I don't know what I want her to say, but I need to talk some more. "My father started to yell at the cops — why weren't there more patrols in the neighborhood," I rattle on, "how the neighborhood isn't safe for decent citizens. I could hear him shouting all the way upstairs. Then I came downstairs and the cops asked me a few questions, but I couldn't help them much. When they left, my father started in on me again — why I had to give the guy all the money. That's all he cared about — the money."

Lana still doesn't say anything, but seems absorbed in her knitting. I feel like shaking her. "Did you hear me?" I say finally.

She puts down her sweater, touches my hand, and looks straight at me. "Well, what did you expect?" she asks.

"I don't know. He could have asked about me, about whether I was all right." Why am I telling this stupid girl all this?

Lana smiles and says, "You look all right to me. No scars or bruises. Any internal bleeding? You don't seem to be leaking anywhere."

"Very funny," I say pulling my hand away.

"No, Richie, you're missing the point," she says. "The robbery didn't upset you. Your father's reaction did."

"Huh?" I stare at her.

"Did you tell your father you were upset with him?" she asks.

"No, of course not. What good would that have done? He was ready to kill me."

"I'm just trying to show you why you're so upset now." she explains.

"I'm not upset," I say, getting upset. "What is this? Are you a psychiatrist? You don't understand at all."

I can see Mrs. Resnick walking over. "Is there a problem?" she asks. "I will have to ask you to keep your voices down if you want to stay here."

"Sorry," I say to her, and she goes back to her desk.

"Calm down, Richie, I understand all right," Lana says. "It's really quite simple. You just felt abandoned at a time of great need. Actually, it's the condition of twentieth-century man, if you read some philosophy."

"Well, I haven't read any philosophy," I say in an angry, low voice. "How come you're such an authority? You don't know my father. I suppose you grew up with the Waltons."

Lana laughs out loud and says, "Hardly. My father lives with some woman in Florida. I don't see him much; he's a pilot. My mother's a doctor. I don't see her much either. When I do, she charges me for a house call."

"What?"

"That's a joke, Richie," Lana says. "Lighten up. I just read a lot, that's all. That's how come I know so much; but aside from that I've learned to trust my instincts, and my instincts tell me you're making too much of this robbery bit. Everybody gets ripped off nowadays. What you have to learn is how to deal with your father."

I don't know what to say. "Eric Edelstein thinks you're crazy."

"Who?"

"Eric Edelstein. He's in your shop class." I pause. "Did you really say that about bookends and God the other day in class?"

"I see news travels fast around here. What does he look like?"

"He usually wears camouflage and reads *Soldier of Fortune*."

60

"Oh, him. Let me see if I can get him." She suddenly stands up straight, salutes with one hand, and with the other brushes imaginary hair out of her eyes. "Eric Edelstein, present and accounted for, sir!" she barks, accentuating heavily the last syllable. She sits down when Mrs. Resnick gives her an exasperated look. "Now that's somebody who's strange," Lana says, giggling. "What is he, sixteen or seventeen, and he's still playing toy soldier?"

"He's my friend," I say in Eric's defense.

"Okay, then, your strange friend. No offense," Lana says. "Listen, Richie, all I'm saying is that you have to get in touch with your feelings and act on them."

"Are you going to be a doctor too? Where'd you pick up all your insight — *People* magazine?" She doesn't have any right to pick on Eric; she doesn't even know him.

"I told you I read a lot," Lana says. "Besides, I've gone to some of the best therapists in the country. The one I had in Florida hardly spoke a word of English, but she understood me. She operated mostly on the affective domain, you know, feelings."

"I don't know," I say. "I don't know what you're talking about half the time. How can one person really know what another person is feeling? It's impossible. You can live in the same house with somebody and not know him at all."

"Like your father?" she asks.

"Look, will you cut that out? Quit trying to psycho-analyze me," I say, my voice rising again.

"It's tough getting through to you," she says.

"Nobody asked you to try," I snap back.

"Richie, I don't give up. But I can see that this particular conversation is getting counterproductive. Maybe when the vibes are better I'll — " But Lana is interrupted.

"All right, you two, that's enough." Mrs. Resnick stands there, her arms crossed. "I've tried to be patient, but I'm afraid you've carried on too loudly. So I'll have to ask you to leave for today. You can come back tomorrow if you promise to keep it down."

Lana looks like she is going to say something to Mrs. Resnick, but decides not to. She gathers her things and walks out, leaving me at the table. "Catch you later," she says over her shoulder. "That is, if you still want to talk to me."

I don't answer and she leaves. As I pick up my own books I think, who needs this crazy girl anyway. I decide to cut my last-period class. I can't hack going to some zoo class, not now. Who the hell does she think she is?

Chapter 5

"You're home early for once," my father says when I walk into the luncheonette. There are a few customers in the store, but no mob yet. "I want to talk to you." It means he's gonna tell me something. First Lana, now him.

"We've been robbed again?" I say. I'm really not up to another round of fighting. I go behind the counter and grab a Coke.

"Don't get smart with me. One robbery is enough, thank you, and it's not going to happen again. Come here. I want to explain this new alarm system to you. I had it put in this morning. There's a buzzer under the register and — "

"Dad, can't this wait? I'm really not in the mood."

"No, it can't wait. I'm sick over what happened, not that you seem to care. Money doesn't grow on trees, you know."

I don't say anything back.

He shows me the system, which is not all that complicated. "And there's another thing I want to tell you," he says.

"What is it now?" I say wearily. "What did I do now?"

"It's what you didn't do," he says. "Do you know your school has a college office?"

"Yeah, but —"

"And you didn't tell me?"

A customer comes in and asks for two cigars. My father goes and gets them. I grab a newspaper and scan the headlines. Saved by the bell.

"Don't you care about your education?" he says after the customer leaves. I'm wrong; he's still after me, bell or no bell.

"Not particularly," I say, reaching for a Milky Way.

"That's what I figured. So I made an appointment for you with the college office, day after tomorrow. Room 318. Here's the information." He hands me a piece of paper.

"I don't believe you did that. You called up the school?"

"What's wrong with that?"

"It's embarrassing. I'm not a baby."

"Stop acting like one, then. You weren't doing nothing, so I had to find out some information, something you should have done on your own."

"I don't believe you really did that."

My father throws some dishes in the sink. "Somebody's got to light a fire under you, kid," he says. "You spend

64

your whole life watching those stupid TV programs and nothing ever gets done. You need an education. What happens if I die or something. How are you gonna take care of yourself?"

"Stop talking like that. You're gonna live a long time."

"So why do you try to shorten my life? Go to the interview."

Just then more customers come in. "See what they want," my father says.

As I put a couple of hamburgers on the grill, I think about my father and all his orders. And now he's trying to make me feel guilty. Well, I'm not going to that interview. Let my father go if he's so damn interested.

"Hey, kid, put up a hamburger for me and make it rare. Don't burn it like you usually do."

That raspy voice belongs to Stanley. He is one of my father's oldest customers as well as his good friend. I hate him.

Stanley drops in at least once a day; his meat store is a few doors down the block. Same order all the time: hamburger, rare, and a chocolate malted. I like making malteds. The trick is to use the coldest milk possible. For Stanley, however, I'm tempted to boil the milk.

Why this feeling for Stanley? Simple. Stanley was my Little League baseball coach years ago when my father forced me to play. "Make a ball player out of him," my father had said to his friend. I was ten years old at the time, but I still remember the conversation with Stanley.

"What position do you want to play?" Stanley asked.

"I don't care," I said.

"What about first base? You're big enough."

"It doesn't matter."

"Don't you like baseball?"

"I like swimming better."

"Well, you gotta play someplace."

"How about my room? It's cooler there."

"C'mon, your father asked me to put you on the team. Know anything about the outfield?"

"It's behind the infield?"

"I think I'll put you in right field. If a ball comes near, you let the center fielder handle it."

I remember one game in particular. I felt like a fool with Stanley's Meat Market printed on my shirt. My "stats" for the game: two ground balls that ran through my legs for home runs; one fly ball that landed thirty feet behind me; three strikeouts as I stood at home plate with the bat on my shoulder praying for a walk; and, finally, having an eight-year-old pinch-hit for me. Embarrassing.

I make the malted anyway, with cold milk.

"Richie, make up some of the Sunday papers now," my father calls. "Some of the sections are already in."

I hate making up the papers; it's the most boring job I know.

"Get a move on," my father says irritably. The bundles are heavy, I need a crane.

Stanley turns around to me and says, "How's my old right fielder?"

"Fine," I say, hoping he won't say more, but he adds, "Catch any fly balls recently?" Stanley loves to give me

66

the needle. I don't say anything, but I'm getting pretty steamed up.

"You see Charlie much?" Stanley asks when I don't answer him. Charlie is Stanley's son, a conceited jock who is six-foot three, has muscles like trees, and a football helmet for a brain. Thank God I don't have classes with that jerk this term. "Not much," I say.

Stanley doesn't give up. "Hey, all-star, where you goin' to school next year? Maybe you and Charlie will go to the same school, maybe even be roommates."

Fat chance, I think as I pour his malted in a large glass. Charlie, no doubt, will be going to some jock heaven like Neanderthal State, where he will play football and major in tying his own shoelaces.

"So where's it gonna be?" he says, slurping his malted. "UCLA? Michigan State? They have some great teams there."

"I don't know," I say, wondering if I could accidentally on purpose knock over his malted into his lap.

"You look pale," Stanley persists. "You've got to get out and grab some fresh air. Why don't you go down to the 'Y' and work out a bit? It'll put some meat on your bones."

"Sometimes I go swimming there. . . ." I start to say before my father interrupts.

"Leave the kid alone, Stanley; he's got to finish up the papers. Worry about your own kid."

"My Charlie?" Stanley answers. "He's an ace. Never gave me a day of trouble in his whole life. You should see the girls hangin' all over him. Doesn't Richie like girls?"

I'm ready to hit Stanley. He sees the look on my face and backs off. "Only kidding, tiger. Sam, your kid doesn't have a sense of humor, does he? I just wanted to find out what college he's going to."

"Stanley," my father says sharply, "you want something else? I'm busy. The kid's got a college interview comin' up, okay?"

I feel my father's ashamed of me. I don't like most sports, I don't have girls hanging all over me, and I'm not going to UCLA.

"Dad, the papers are finished," I say. I gotta get out of here, go for a walk or something before I put my fist through a wall. I think of going to the "Y" for a cool swim.

"Be back soon, I may need you."

No time for a swim, then.

My head is pounding. Let Charlie be my father's son, then.

Of course I like girls — blonds, brunettes, redheads. But where are they? I haven't met anyone really special yet. The girls in my class only go out with college guys and all the rest are babies.

What if I pack a suitcase and just leave — leave school, the store, everything — and walk into a newspaper office in a town where they never heard of me. I'd work my way up to lead stories on the front page with *my* by-line. Nobody would hassle me about college, my love life, or anything. What love life?

I walk around the block. I really feel confused. The same thoughts spin around in my head. I'm in a tunnel

68

and people are holding up signs: Go to College, Work in the Store, Find a Girl, Be a Jock

They can all go to hell.

I sit on a fire hydrant and watch the cars go by; the people in them, no doubt, seem to know where they're going.

"Hey, Richie, over here." I look down the street and see Eric skipping toward me – skipping, would you believe.

"What's with you?" I ask when he reaches me and practically steps on my foot.

"Richie, my boy, I'm in love, I'm in love," he laughs, grinning like an idiot.

"With what – a machine gun?"

"Funny man," he says, punching me lightly on the shoulder. "No, dodo, a real live one. I met her yesterday after gym in the lunch line. In Ptomaine Alley I met my true love." I have never seen Eric so happy, not even when he's talking about nuclear destruction.

"It was beautiful, man," he goes on, "just like in the movies. We both reached for an orange at the same time and then I got to talking to her. Just like that. She asked me about my *Soldier of Fortune* magazine. Richie, it was wonderful." He pushes me away from the hydrant, steps on top of it and screams out loud, "I love everybody!"

"You're kidding," I say. "You met someone as crazy as you? Impossible."

He jumps off the hydrant, fakes a few playful punches at me and says, "I swear to God it's true. She's an army brat, just got transferred here. Her name is Venezia Paris.

Isn't that a beautiful name? The girl is bright, sexy, and all army. I want her to have my children."

"Eric, you're crazy. You just met this girl," I say. What I feel, though, is jealousy. Even Edelstein has made it. What's wrong with me?

"Crazy in love, my man. Wait till you meet her. God, is she built, what a body! We've got to find someone for you; maybe she has a friend. Then we can double date, go to air shows together."

"Air shows?" I say.

"Sure. Venezia's old man is some sort of a test pilot. I'm going over to her house now."

"When did all this happen?" I ask, sitting down on the hydrant.

"Yesterday, I told you. After I saw you. I didn't go to the shopping center. I had to go back to school because I left my wallet in my locker. Then I got hungry and went to the lunchroom. Do you believe in fate? Venezia and I spent the whole day talking about military history. What a mind that girl has — incredible! She invited me to dinner with her folks. Her family's been everywhere, you name it — the Far East, Africa, South America. You should hear the stories her old man tells."

"I hear enough stories from my old man," I say sourly.

"Look, I gotta get over to Venezia's house now; she's expecting me. Want to come?"

"No, I have to get back to work. I'm sure my father will call out the National Guard if I don't get back soon."

"Still on a leash, I see," he says with a smile.

I feel like punching him. "Look, Edelstein," I explode,

"just because you lucked out all of a sudden, don't think you can come around here and brag about your military conquests. You can go to – "

"Hold up, man," he says grabbing my shoulder. "Sorry, no offense. I just want the whole world to feel great, that's all."

"I gotta get back," I say.

"Well, I'll see you soon," he says. "Stay loose."

"Yeah."

He goes off and I start back for the store. Life is all luck. Maybe I should start eating lunch in school. Wonderful. My own true love is waiting behind an egg salad sandwich.

When I walk back into the luncheonette, my father gives me a what-did-you-take-so-long-for look. I don't say anything, but go right to the sink where another stack of dirty dishes is waiting for me. I want to take the whole pile of them and smash them against the wall.

I bet Venezia looks like a landing barge, anyway. Who's he kidding? The great Major Captain Colonel Romeo Casanova Edelstein, a legend in his own mind.

"Hey, Richie," my father calls to me, "two coffees to travel, one with no sugar, and a tuna on rye, hold the mayo."

NBC News capsule: Galley slave fills one millionth cup of coffee. Details at eleven. Now back to our regular programming.

The next day in English, Mrs. Fabrikant, with her nice voice, stands in front of the room and tries to introduce *The Grapes of Wrath*. The class wants to hang out and nod off. One sleepy kid in the back of the room opens his eyes wide enough to see that the novel is five hundred pages and yells out, "You actually expect me to read this?"

"You'll love it," Mrs. Fabrikant calmly assures him. "It's one of the great books of the twentieth century." The kid goes back to sleep.

Eric shows me the rocket silos he's drawing. "The MX missile plan is definitely nonoperational. There are serious design flaws in the system," he says.

"Can anyone tell me what the Great Depression was?" Mrs. Fabrikant asks. "How about you — she looks in her roll book — Eric Edelstein?"

"I didn't hear you, ma'am," he says, buying time and turning over his rocket drawing. "Can you repeat the question?"

"Can you tell me what the Great Depression was?"

"No, ma'am. I wasn't around then," Eric says.

"Anyone else?"

"When I broke up with my boyfriend," a girl shouts from the back.

Mrs. Fabrikant gives a long sigh, goes to her desk and picks up some photographs. The houses pictured are surrounded by dust and tilt at crazy angles.

"Hey, that looks like your house, Danny," the kid in front of me says to the guy on his right.

"No way, man — your mother's. See the customers coming out?"

A fight breaks out, mostly shoves and pushes, that drives Mrs. Fabrikant out into the hall to get the security guards. They materialize in a couple of seconds and haul the two pugilists down to the dean.

Yes, we have security guards. School safety officers, they call themselves — huge football types who man the halls with their walkie-talkies saying weird things like, "Roger, base one, over." Eric says they're not exactly the Green Berets.

Mrs. Fabrikant, shaken after the fight, asks the class to read chapter one on their own. The first few pages are boring. Who wants to read about all that red dust?

I am an expert on fights. My thoughts drift back, all the way back to River Lake Nursery School and my first day of school. I didn't go without a fight. A pattern for all the other days? I wonder.

"Can I watch TV there?" I asked.

"I don't think so," my mother said, tying my shoe-laces.

"What about swimming? Do they have a swimming pool there?"

"I'm afraid not, honey," she said.

"Then what will I do?"

"There's lots to do. You'll play with the other kids, build blocks, paint pictures, lots of things."

"That stuff's boring."

"Richie, darling, you'll love it, you'll see. You'll make lots of new friends."

"Why can't I stay here in the house?" I asked.

"You know you can't do that. Your father's working in the store and I have class. There's nobody to watch you."

"I can watch myself. The TV can watch me. I'm not going."

"Yes, you are. It's all settled," my father said, coming into my room. "We paid for it already."

"Nobody asked me, no fair."

"Too bad," my father said, "you're going."

I kicked and screamed and turned over a table in my room.

Next morning I was on the bus and after twenty minutes of bouncing on the seat, which almost made me throw up, I arrived at River Lake Nursery School. I hated it right away.

A large lady, who didn't look at all like the lady from "Sesame Street" on TV, met me at the door and took me down a long, green hallway that had cubbyholes on each side. At the end of the hallway was a large room with a painting corner, two different building-block areas, and in the center a large round table with many chairs. Yuck. The only interesting thing in the place was a water table; it was like a shallow bathtub where you could play with boats and things.

"Is there something you want to play with?" Miss Rosalie asked. She looked like a fat clown.

"Where's the TV set?"

"I'm afraid we don't have one. Maybe you'd like to play with one of the other boys. See Thomas over there? Do you want to see what he's doing?"

"No." Thomas looked as large as Miss Rosalie. He was banging two wooden trucks together.

"Maybe you'd like a book from our library corner?"

74

Miss Rosalie said, trying to smile. I didn't say anything, but she gave me a book anyway, pushing me into a seat before breaking up a fight between two girls who were throwing tea cups at each other.

I hated the place. I put my head in my arms and went to sleep.

Miss Rosalie woke me for snack time. It was awful — carrots that looked brown. I felt like throwing up again.

Later, I played a bit at the water table. I pretended that I was swimming with my mother. Miss Rosalie came over to me. I wished she'd leave me alone. "You're here to have fun," she said. "Maybe we can find something to amuse you. Let's look in the toy box."

I saw an Etch-a-Sketch. It looked like a small portable TV. I played with it for a long time, making the lines go this way and that.

I heard footsteps near me. Large Thomas stood over me. He smelled awful. "I wanna play with that," he said.

"No," I said, making more lines.

"It's my turn. Give it to me."

I held on to my Etch-a-Sketch more tightly.

"If you don't I'll punch you in the nose," he said.

I looked quickly for Miss Rosalie. She was getting some Play-Doh out of a girl's hair.

"I want that," Thomas said meanly.

"No," I said, frightened.

He punched me; blood came out of my nose, lots of it, all over my face. "I want my Sketchy! Mommy, help me!" I cried through the blood and the tears.

The memory of that first day still bothers me as I sit in

my English class wondering how many minutes are left in the period. I think they designed school purposely to include long bouts of boredom punctuated by moments of terror. In the sixth grade my lunch money was stolen for a week by some cretin, no doubt a relative of Large Thomas. Junior high was the worst, the "Pubic Wars" I heard one teacher describe it. In high school I can breathe more easily, but I have to be careful. I never carry too much money with me and never put anything important in my locker.

What am I thinking of all this junk for? Doesn't the bell ever ring?

Eric has given up reading and is drawing something new. "What is that?" I ask.

"A rocket motorcycle complete with mounted Uzi machine guns," he says matter-of-factly.

"Looks like something out of James Bond," I say.

"I'm gonna give this picture to Venezia," he says, beaming.

"What are you going to give her for her birthday — a grenade?"

"You just don't understand love, Richie," he says, brushing the hair out of his eyes.

"Where is this phantom militia woman? I think she's a figment of your warped imagination."

"Just you wait. You'll see her soon enough — and don't get any ideas — she's mine."

The bell finally rings and Eric and I go off to gym. "Are you ready for some serious basketball?" he says. It may be Eric's favorite period, but it's certainly not mine. The only good thing about it is that next period I get to see Ms. Poquette.

After gym I head for typing and the poetic loveliness of Ms. Poquette. I wonder how old she is. She can't be that much older than me.

Only she is not there. My day is ruined. Half the class cuts out on the substitute. I spend the time writing in my book.

"Listen, I'm sorry about the other day," Lana says as she drops her book bag and a tennis racket on the library table. "I have a rotten habit of butting into other people's lives. Forgive me?" She smiles. Lana is dressed in a lavender sweat suit with a matching headband. Why can't she dress like a normal human being. Her bag covers my writing book.

"I don't know what gets into me," she says, pulling two large Granola bars from her bag. "Forgot to eat today. You want one?"

"No thanks."

"My new shrink says I come on too strong to people. My need for attention, he calls it. Somebody listens to me for a second and I instantly try to rearrange him. Sorry."

"Forget about it," I say. "How come the new outfit? What happened to the *Vogue* model?"

"A new dodge," she says lightly. "I figure it will keep my mother off my back for a while, clotheswise. This way I can look both sloppy and 'in,' if you know what I mean. I told my mother I was trying out for the tennis team. She practically jumped for joy, said I was trying hard to make new friends, a welcome change, she thought. Sure you don't want a Granola bar?"

"I didn't know you knew how to play tennis."

"I don't, but I guess I can fake it. Just grab the racket and make like Chris Evert." She hits the racket with the flat part of her hand.

"Evert-Lloyd. I think she's married," I say.

"Evert-Lloyd, then. What's the difference? My mother doesn't know a forehand from a backhand. She just wants me to become part of a group, figures it will aid my social development. She's not the type to come down to practice anyway, much too busy. We leave notes for each other on a bulletin board on the side of the refrigerator—the correspondence school of parental involvement." She plucks the strings of her racket. "Isn't this a weird-looking banjo?" she says.

"But at least you can talk to your parents," I say.

"Oh, sure. By long distance. You're lucky; your father's around. You at least work with him."

"Big deal. He's always talking about baseball. He should do the color commentary for the networks."

"Talk to him about baseball, then. It doesn't matter. At least your father's not a thousand miles away, acting out some fantasy with some girl who's barely older than I am."

"Right now all he wants to talk about is college. He's driving me crazy. He even made an appointment for me with the college office."

Lana puts down her racket and looks at me. "What's wrong with that?" she asks.

"It's the principle of the thing."

"What principle? He wants you to go to college. That hardly qualifies as parental abuse."

"It's more than that. You don't understand."

"What's the big deal? It's not a crime to do something your father wants. Go to the appointment, make him happy; it's no skin off your nose. I wish my father were around to help me," she says, suddenly getting misty. "I miss him, I miss him a lot." She takes a big red handkerchief out of her book bag and loudly blows her nose. I see people at other tables turning around. "Sorry," she says, "I always get choked up when I think about my father."

"Are you going to college?" I ask stupidly, trying to change the subject. I never met anyone whose mood changed so quickly.

"You bet," she says, brightening. "As soon as I get out of here I'm gonna pop in on my old man and get rid of the parasite he's living with. It'll be nice — me and him fishing off the coast. But college? Sure thing. Aren't you going?"

"No, I've been thinking of doing something else, actually."

She picks up my notebook from under her bag and reads: Richie Linder, Writing Book. "I bet it has to do with this," she says, holding it up.

"You've been looking in my book," I say grabbing it back. "I don't want anyone to see it."

"Back off, will ya, I haven't touched your precious book. I just got here, remember? Paranoid City, I swear.

You're worse than I am. So you're a closet writer, so what? If I could write, I'd be knocking on the door of every publishing house in the city. Your stuff any good?"

"It's not good enough."

"How do you know that?"

"I just know, that's all."

"Wonderful," she says, "just wonderful. If Shakespeare had said that, we never would have had his plays. Don't you just love *Romeo and Juliet*? So beautiful, so tragic."

"I'm not Shakespeare."

"Then be you," she says. "Listen, I gotta go now. What time is it? I made an appointment to practice with some of the girls."

"I thought you didn't know how to play tennis."

"I'm not going to let a little detail like that get in the way. Gotta keep Dr. Mommy happy. See you later. By the way, do you like camping?"

"What?"

"Just a thought. Keep it in mind. Go write me a beautiful poem. Ta-ta. Please be good enough to point me in the direction of Wimbledon."

She gathers up her book bag and racket and walks to the door of the library. Just before she leaves she yells out, "Tennis, anyone?" and is out the door before Mrs. Resnick can say anything.

I scrunch lower in my seat. Mrs. Resnick looks at me angrily, but she doesn't say a word. I don't look back at her. I'm too embarrassed, guilty by association.

I don't feel like going to my last-period class. I'd rather write in my book.

I see a couple holding hands across a table, not far from where I'm sitting. Everybody's got someone, I think. Even Edelstein, or so he says. What am I stuck with? — a crazy girl in a lavender sweat suit who yells out, "Tennis, anyone?" Great, just great.

Camping?

Chapter 6

WHEN I GET HOME Ernie peers out from behind the register and nods hello. Ernie doesn't say much, but he eats a lot. He's always munching on a roll or something. You'd think he'd weigh as much as a horse, but he's the skinniest man I have ever seen. My father hired him about six years ago, a friend of a friend sort of thing. I still don't know too much about him other than the fact he lives in the neighborhood and cares for a sick mother. Ernie hardly says more than one sentence at a time. He's about forty-five or so, but it's hard to tell. A couple of customers sit at the counter.

"Hi, Ernie. Where's my father?" I ask.

"Out in back."

"What's he doing?"

"I don't know."

End of the conversation. I take a *TV Guide* from

the rack and start doing the crossword puzzle. I can do them in five minutes.

"You and the old man have a fight?" Ernie asks. It's not like him to say anything that doesn't have to do directly with store business.

"What did he say?" I ask.

"Nothing, not a word, but he called me Richie a couple of times."

"Maybe the robbery is still bothering him," I say, but I know the real reason has less to do with the robbery than with me and my future.

"Maybe," Ernie says.

I go into the back storeroom and see my father checking some invoices for two large crates that apparently just came in.

"What's in the boxes, Dad — refrigerators?"

"You'll see as soon as I open them up. Hand me those clippers over there," he growls. *"Talk to him."* Lana's words come back to me. How can I talk to him when all he does is bark orders?

I hand him the clippers and he snaps the wires and opens the crates. Inside are two electronic arcade games. He puts one of the games on a hand truck and wheels it to the space where the fourth booth was to have been built, but never was.

"Let me give you a hand with that, Dad," I say.

"I don't need no help," he says, dismissing me with a wave of his hand. "I'm as strong as an ox."

And stubborn as a mule, I think.

"Ernie," he yells. "Go sweep up in back. It's a mess."

"Okay," Ernie says and nothing more.

"Ernie is a good worker," my father says, sweating over the hand truck. What my father doesn't say is "compared to other people I know."

"You got Dragon's Lair?" I say to my father as he plugs in the machine.

"Naah," he says, not looking at me. "Better than that. This little beauty is Body Count and the other one in the crate is Jet Age Baseball."

"Body Count?"

"A great little war game. You try to shoot as many soldiers coming over the hill as you can before the enemy tank gets you. Great idea, no?"

"I didn't know we're turning the luncheonette into an arcade," I say, trying to make a joke. He doesn't even smile. "I didn't think business was that slow."

"Of course it's slow," he says. "Shows you how much you pay attention to things around here."

I ignore the dig. "Think it'll help?" I say.

"Can't hurt," he says, wiping the screen with a dry cloth. "Kids all over the country play these things, or haven't you noticed; adults too."

"I'm not sure it's a good idea," I say.

"Who asked you?" he says, turning around. "I'm not asking you to do nothing, just keep your eyes on the machines once in a blue moon. It's just like TV; you should love it."

Another dig.

"You want me to get the other machine?" I ask.

"No, I'll get it later when Ernie's finished up."

84

For some perverse reason, maybe because we're actually having some sort of conversation, I ask him, "Dad, why did you drop out of school?"

"Because I was stupid," he says.

"No, really. Didn't anyone try to make you stay?"

"Sure. My old man. Only I didn't have enough sense to listen to him. You never really knew your grandfather, kid. He was quite a man; hardly missed a day of work in his life. All he said was, 'You're making a mistake,' and he was right."

A customer comes in and orders a roast beef on rye. My father goes and puts a hunk of meat on the slicing machine. "It was a good thing they cut me at the end of the season; otherwise I might have gone on fooling myself."

I see an opening. Not that I want round three, but it's so obvious. "Why don't you give me a chance to make my own mistakes, like you did?" I say.

My father turns off the machine, slaps the meat between two pieces of rye and practically throws it at the customer. He grabs my arm, pulls me into a corner and whispers fiercely, "Are you starting that crap again about dropping out? I'm warning you. You're going to college and that's final, you hear? Didn't you go to that appointment I made for you?"

"It's for tomorrow," I say. He's hurting my arm.

"Well, make sure that you keep it," he says, letting go of me.

Ernie returns from the back room. "Storeroom's okay," he says.

"Fine," my father says. "Whaddya taking off your apron for?"

"Got to take my mother to the doctor."

"What, again?"

"Yep."

"Go ahead, then," my father says irritably. "See you tomorrow."

"Okay, boss."

My father turns to me. "I'll get the other machine," he says. "You handle the customers. I also need some more potatoes cut up and cooked. And put on a clean apron."

He gets the baseball machine and installs it next to Body Count. Then he joins me behind the counter. He seems like a dancer dashing back and forth serving people, clearing dishes, all the while keeping up a constant stream of chatter with the customers. He must have been a very talkative catcher.

The new machines are already attracting a crowd. Two barbarians with studded jackets hover over Body Count. My father yells at me from the end of the counter to get two English muffins and a Sanka.

I'm putting up the muffins when I hear a familiar voice call out, "Didn't see you in history, buddy boy." It's Eric with a girl attached to his arm. "It's not so bad now. Mr. Whitaker got rid of a few goons. The class is much better now."

"I didn't feel like going," I say quietly because I don't want my father to hear that. The girl with Eric is drop-dead beautiful.

86

"Two Cokes, please, *garçon*," Eric says grandly. "Don't worry, I got the bread."

I stare at the girl, who is dressed in a green army jacket just like Eric's. A matched pair they are. She sees me staring and lowers her eyes.

"Oh, *excusez-moi*," Eric says. "I forgot. Richie, this is Venezia Paris, the love of my life, the mother of my future children. Isn't she the most gorgeous girl you've ever seen?"

Venezia punches Eric on the shoulder. "You're embarrassing me — stop," she says, giggling softly.

"Hi," I say.

"Hi," she says back.

There is a long pause. I don't know what to say. Venezia is as pretty as Ms. Poquette.

"You want something to eat?" Eric says to Venezia. "Richie makes a mean hamburger."

"No, thank you," Venezia says politely.

"Hi, Mr. Linder," Eric says to my father, who barely acknowledges Eric's wave, but stares for a second at Venezia. Then he goes back to the customers in the store.

Eric says, "I'm walking Venezia home. She's gonna help me with my math homework. And I love figures." He looks over at Venezia, but she doesn't respond to his little joke. Neither do I.

"Oh, by the way," Eric says, "I bumped into that weirdo friend of yours, what's her name, Lana? Outside of school. Where was she going — to a costume party? A purple sweat suit — come on, really."

"Don't call her weird," I say sharply. "She's very nice."

"Whatever you say, champ," he says. "You two got something going?"

"No," I say, looking at Venezia.

Eric and Venezia finish their Cokes. She catches me staring at her again. "It's been very nice meeting you," she says after Eric pays for the drinks. "Bye." They walk off together in step.

My father walks over to me and says, "Who's the girl with Eric — his sister?"

"No, his girlfriend," I say.

"I wish you could find a girl like that," my father says, taking Eric's change off the counter. "She's a real looker."

Right, Dad. Sure, I think. Bring on the beauties, the Miss America Pageant live from Linder's Luncheonette. Count 'em. Fifty gorgeous girls all crowding around me, tearing at my clothes and running their fingers through my hair. And wearing the diamond tiara, Ms. Poquette (first runner-up, Venezia Paris) — scintillating, sexy, soft Ms. Poquette, wearing my high-school ring (if I had one) and my varsity jacket (also if I had one). "She *is* pretty," I say to my father. I wish I could find someone like her too.

Just then the pay phone rings. Probably some supplier for my father. They're always calling up and making excuses about late orders.

"It's for you," my father says. "Make it short. The phone's for the customers, not you."

"For me?" I say, taking the receiver from him. I never get calls.

"Hello?" I say.

"Meet me at Gorman's in a half hour. I'm in trouble."

"Who's this?" I say, not recognizing the voice.

"Mata Hari," the voice says in a thick German accent with a southern lilt to it.

"Lana?"

"*Sehr gut*. I need your help right away. It's a matter of extreme urgency," she says.

"What's wrong?"

"I can't tell you over the phone. Spies might be listening. Just hurry. Gorman's Sports Store in the shopping center. Know where it is?"

"Yeah, sure, but . . ."

"Hurry! It's an emergency. I need you." The phone clicks dead.

I stand there holding the receiver. Without thinking about it too much I quickly take off my apron and say to my father, "A friend of mine's in trouble. I gotta go."

"What, are you crazy? You can't leave now," he says.

"I gotta, Dad, it's an emergency," I say, rushing to the register for some change for the bus.

"Richie, you come back," my father calls, but I'm already out the door.

On the bus I try to think what kind of trouble she could be in. Is she hurt? Did she get arrested for shoplifting? And why did she call me? More important, why am I going?

The bus makes good time to the shopping center. I race past some stores over to Gorman's. I don't see her at first. Maybe she's in the hospital. Maybe the police have already taken her away.

I feel a tap on my shoulder and turn around to see Lana munching on an ice-cream cone. "Marble swirl fudge, delicious, but drippy," she says, wiping her hands on her sweat shirt. She is also wearing a blue baseball cap. "What kept you?" she says.

"Are you all right?" I ask quickly.

"Sure, I'm all right," she says, smiling. "You want some ice cream? I hate pigging out by myself."

"What's the emergency?"

"No emergency. I just wanted company while I do a little shopping."

"What?" I say, my mouth dropping open in surprise. "You call me up — How'd you get my number?"

"New invention. The telephone book. Very handy."

"Right. You call me up, give me some crazy story how it's a matter of life and death. I race down here like a maniac and you just want company for shopping?"

"That's about the size of it," she says. "Would you have come otherwise? I had to ham it up a bit, hope you don't mind. You're a true friend."

"I don't believe you," I say, but I start laughing.

"What are you laughing at?" Lana says. "At me?"

"No, at what my father would say if I told him."

"Don't tell him, then. Look upon it as an extended coffee break."

Lana finishes her ice cream, takes my arm and we walk into Gorman's. It's a pretty big store, with different sections for different sports.

We walk past the baseball gloves and bats, and I think for a second of that first game with my father. "We need a few supplies for our trip," Lana says.

"Trip? What trip?" I ask.

"I told you, dummy. The camping trip we're going on."

"You're joking," I say.

"I am not joking, Richie. This is serious business. What do you know about kerosene lamps?"

"Nothing, not a thing. I've never gone camping in my life."

"All the more reason for the trip, then," she says, pulling me toward the camping section. She picks up a big ax and says, "Let me ax you a question. Don't you want to go camping with me?"

"I really haven't given it much thought. Wouldn't a movie be easier? I mean, don't you need all kinds of gear for that? Tents, sleeping bags, food?"

"Don't sweat it. I have all that junk. We just have to pick up a few odds and ends, that's all."

"You want to go camping with me?" I ask.

"What are you, slow or something? Yes, I want to go camping with you." She picks up a hunting knife and gingerly touches the blade.

"I'm not exactly Daniel Boone."

"I'm not asking for Marco Polo either. Just a little trip upstate. What do you say?" she asks sweetly.

"I don't know if I can get away — you know, the store. I had trouble getting out now to meet you."

Lana puts the knife back on the rack and looks at me,

her smile vanishing. "What do you need, for God's sake, a permission slip from your father? Listen, I'll drop by the luncheonette tomorrow, I know where it is, and you can tell me then if I have a trail partner or not." She walks away from me, like an actress exiting the stage, and goes down another aisle.

I'd like to go camping, I think, but with her? I turn the corner of the aisle. Lana is looking at the kerosene lamps.

"If we did go, how are we going to get there?" I ask. "I don't have a car."

"Just leave that to me," she says. "What do you think about this lamp? It's on sale."

"Looks okay," I say.

"And we'll need a compass," she adds. "Oh, Richie, I'm so excited about this trip. It'll be great fun, guaranteed. I even have an extra sleeping bag."

I raise an eyebrow.

"Not that kind of fun, you lech," she says. "This is going to be a perfectly innocent return to Mother Nature. A grab in the night I can always get. This is going to be one terrific weekend, I just know it!"

I'm unprepared for the big hug she suddenly gives me, so unprepared that we both fall over into a rack of fishing poles. The poles go flying every which way. Lana comes up laughing; I come up embarrassed.

A salesman rushes over and asks icily if we want to buy anything or are we just content to destroy everything in the store. Lana looks at all the fishing poles scattered about like pick-up sticks and laughs even louder. Other people in the store turn and stare. I want to crawl into a hole.

"Let's get out of here," I say, pulling at Lana's arm.

"In a sec, Richie. Let me pay for the lamp and the compass." She reaches down in her jeans, pulls out some money and pays the clerk. "I'd like it gift wrapped. It's a present for me," she says. The clerk gives her a strange look. I hurry out of the store.

Outside, Lana catches up to me, the lamp swinging in her hand and says, "I embarrassed you in there, didn't I?" I don't say anything. Yes, you did, I think.

"Oh, Richie, you're such a stuffed shirt. Loosen up. That was a panic in there."

Maybe going camping with her is not such a great idea. "Maybe we should forget about this trip," I say, "if that's the way you feel."

"What are you talking about?" Lana says. "We're a great team — Mr. Normal and Miss Neurotic. Listen, Linder, in case you haven't gotten the message yet, I like you, God knows why. You're nice; you put up with me, even if I do tend to cause a few scenes, an old habit of mine. You don't know how much I appreciate that. It hasn't been easy for me here. Most people seem to think I'm a complete kook — not you. You're a rock, you know that? I don't want to get too maudlin about this, but you're my friend and good friends are hard to come by."

"Well, you're my friend too," I say tentatively.

"Well, don't get so emotional about it," she says sarcastically. "Hey, I'm starved. Let's grab something to eat. Isn't there a pizza joint or something around here?"

We walk into Carmine's Pizza Palace a few stores down. "My treat," Lana says. "What do you want?"

"A slice and a Coke, I guess," I say.

"How boring," Lana says. She calls to the guy behind the counter, "Two slices and two Cokes, please, and put plenty of anchovies on my piece." To me she says, "Don't you just love anchovies?"

"I think they look like worms," I say.

"That's what I like about you, Richie. You have the soul of a poet. And speaking of same, how's your writing coming along?"

"I haven't been doing much lately."

"But you have to, really have to. I feel it's gonna be your connection to immortality. Say, doesn't the school have a newspaper or something?"

"Yeah, it comes out once a month, I think."

"Did you ever think of joining it?" she asks.

"Not really. I hear the guy who runs it is real mean, treats his students like slaves and doesn't give them a chance to write anything that's important. Everybody knows Treadwell and how stuck-up he is. Bathroom walls all over the school have suggestions about what he could do with certain parts of his anatomy."

Lana laughs and says, "He sounds like a charmer. So what? Teachers are teachers. You just have to know how to handle them."

"I don't know. I think I'm afraid of the guy."

"Well, I'm not," Lana says, picking an anchovy off

her slice and popping it into her mouth. "Wait and see. Oh, by the way, I ran into your friend Eric outside of school before. He had his arm wrapped around some girl. I thought he just liked military hardware."

"I know. She's very pretty, isn't she?"

"If you like that type," Lana says, pouting. "I'm gonna get another slice. You want?"

"No, no thanks. I really think I should be getting back to the store. My father's gonna have my head."

"What's been the greatest day of your life?" Lana asks suddenly.

Where did that question come from? Lana is like a car that constantly shifts from one gear to another without warning.

"I'm taking a survey," she says, a piece of cheese hanging at the corner of her mouth. "Maybe I'll write a book one day. You think you're the only one with artistic aspirations?"

"I don't know, let me think," I say. But I do know already. I tell her the story of the swimming race at the "Y" camp. "Well, when I was ten my mother sent me for two weeks to the country, to the camp run by the 'Y' around here, you know where it is?"

"Yeah, that big brown building," she says, taking a napkin and wiping off the cheese.

"My father wasn't too thrilled about the idea, but my mother insisted, so I went. There was this long-distance race. I think about a half mile or so from one side of the lake to the other. I volunteered for the race. Everybody in my bunk laughed because they knew I wasn't such a great athlete. But I won the race. The funny part was that the boat with me sank and the counselor fell into the water. That evening I got a special trophy. It's still on a shelf in my room."

Lana raises her soda and says, "I salute the victor. Now let me tell you my best time. See this gorgeous red mop?" Lana pulls at her hair. "My sixth-grade teacher decided I would be the perfect Annie for the school play. I had never acted in a real play before, but Mrs. Allison, my teacher, worked with me after school on my lines and songs. My parents were beginning to fight then, so they didn't pay that much attention to me, and my father was spending more and more time out of the house — his work schedule, he said, but I knew better. The day of the play he said he had to fly to Cleveland and I didn't want to go on then, but my mother said I had to. I did go on; in fact, I was merely great, but the best part of the play was afterwards, when both my mother and father came backstage and the three of us hugged and kissed, kissed and hugged."

"But I thought your father was in Cleveland," I say.

"He had switched flights with another pilot just to see me. He saw the whole play. I didn't even know he was in the audience. I'll always remember that day, the three of us hugging and dancing. It was great. I felt we were a really close family. I forgot for the moment they were fighting all the time."

Lana stares into her Coke and I stare into mine. I don't know what to say after her story. But then as if she has mentally changed channels she says, "You realize, Linder, this has been our first date?"

"What date?" I say, surprised. "You conned me down here for a lamp and a compass. What kind of date is that?"

"A mere technicality," she says. "It's not what you do, Richie, it's who you do it with. Besides, regular dating is such a hassle. Believe me, I've been on plenty of dates. What a bore. Boy spends x money and expects y return on his investment. It's all so, well, calculated. I much prefer to do things as the spirit moves me. It's much more fun that way."

"Does that include wrecking stores?" I say, grinning.

"Whatever happens, happens," she says, shrugging her shoulders.

"Listen," I say, "I really should be going."

"You go ahead," Lana says. "I'm gonna do a little more shopping — girl-type things. See you tomorrow, same old place. Fearless forester, hang tough — the woods await."

She leaves and I head for the bus stop. On the ride home I wish I had my writing book. It helps me sort out my thoughts, and what I'm confused about now is Lana. In the first place, she's loud, insulting, direct, and embarrassing; but she's also funny, sympathetic, intelligent, and zany.

And she likes me.

And I guess I like her too, as a friend, though. But as a date, a relationship? I don't know. Still, she makes me laugh. She's so much on stage, I bet she'd make a wonderful actress. But a relationship with her? That's sort of ridiculous.

When I get home my father pounces all over me. "What do you mean, leaving me like that with all the customers to handle? Who do you think you are that you can just take off any damn time you please. Don't you have any sense at all? I swear, I don't understand what gets into you."

But I am saved from more yelling by a new rush of customers who come in. "I'll deal with you later," he says. "Go put up a couple of grilled cheese sandwiches."

I let his orders now wash over me like so much water. Robotlike, I get all the food he calls for. Maybe it's easier not to fight, I think. The picture of Lana sprawled out on the floor in the middle of a pile of fishing rods replays in my mind. My father never makes me laugh, never.

Later, when the customers leave and we are cleaning up, my father again reminds me about that college appointment the next day. "Don't you get any crazy ideas about skipping out of that," he says. "I'm gonna check on you."

I go upstairs, turn on the TV, and get ready for bed. Sometimes the TV plays all night because I fall asleep before I remember to turn it off. Many times I wake up in the middle of the night and hear the station signing off with the national anthem. This night I have a dream:

The sun is rising, and by the morning light I see a small wooden boat pulled up on the shore of a great ocean. I'm making preparations to get under way. Lana, I know, is waiting for me in London, and if the wind is right and my navigation accurate, I'll make the crossing in good time. I look at the charts in my writing book and know that my plans are correct, but something is holding me back. My father? No, he's opening the store now, putting up the potatoes and onions for the morning breakfast special. I love the smell of bacon as it sizzles on the grill. I have trouble raising the sail. Do I want to leave now with the tide? The harbor is so secure, so cozy; sunlight dances on the water, making bright gold and green circles. There is a hole in the boat. Maybe I can swim across? But I patch it up and climb in. I get caught up in all the lines attached to the sails. . . .

I wake up tangled in the sheets on my bed. The national anthem is playing. I don't know if the small wooden boat with the patched-up hole has managed to get away, out past the barrier reef, onto the wide expanse of the sea.

Chapter 7

INSTEAD OF GOING to the library the next day, I keep my appointment, or rather my father's appointment, with the college office.

"Are you Richie Linder?" the man behind the desk says when I walk in.

I nod.

"Good. You're right on time. I'm Mr. Harris. Be with you in just a sec. Just let me clean up some of the papers here. Your folder is here someplace; I just saw it. Two minutes, okay? I could use a vacuum cleaner. You look around. Your father called the other day, right?"

Don't remind me, I think.

Mr. Harris, the college counselor, looks like a fat teddy bear. He has wire glasses, curly black hair, and is about forty, I'd guess. The office reminds me of an old secondhand bookstore. Papers and folders are scattered everywhere. Catalogues from a million colleges fill a huge bookcase on the back wall. There is a musty lived-in odor, something like the cigars we sell in the store.

Mr. Harris must have read my mind. "Excuse the appearance of this place," he says, "but we are in the middle of converting over to computers. The world according to IBM. I have seen the future and it glows. I read that somewhere. I'm not sure I like the idea of possibly being replaced by a machine. Progress, I guess."

I like him immediately, a definite thumbs-up.

"Now, what can I do for you?" he asks.

"I'm not sure."

"Well, let's look at your folder. It was here a minute ago. God, what a mess." He dives into the papers on his desk. "Here it is," he says. He opens it up. "I think we have a small problem here. The folder's empty. You don't exist," he laughs.

He adjusts his glasses. "You didn't bring your preliminary work sheet, did you?" he says.

"No."

"Three teacher recommendations?"

"No."

"Your autobiography?"

"No."

He leans back in his chair, picks up a sucking candy from a bowl on his desk and pops it into his mouth. "I'm trying to give up smoking," he says. "Now I just get cavities. From the looks of this folder I'd say you have to start high school again."

"What?"

"Only kidding. I wonder, though, didn't you get any of that information we sent out to all the homerooms last term? We really don't have much to go on here. I don't even have your transcript. Do you know your average?"

"About a C," I say.

"That's fair enough. But tell me, Richie, I'm getting the distinct feeling that you're not exactly clear about next year. Am I right? Do you want to go to college?"

"Sometimes I feel I should go to college; most times I don't. It's all very mixed up."

He picks up my folder and writes something in it. "So why did you come to see me?" he asks after a few seconds.

"I don't know for sure," I say.

"Your father made this appointment for you; correct me if I'm wrong."

"Well, yeah," I say, "college is more his idea than mine."

Maybe I could leave now, just walk out of the office, I think. I fully expect Mr. Harris to say something like: Come back when you're ready, but instead he says, "Well, we definitely have a small problem here. Do you have any idea what you want to do after high school? What do you like doing? You know, interests, hobbies?"

I want to tell him that what I'd like to do is walk out of this school right now, that my father can take his college idea and stick it, but I don't think Mr. Harris would understand that. "I like watching television," I say stupidly.

Mr. Harris laughs easily. "You and every other teen-ager I know. You're not a soap opera freak, are you?"

"I like news programs, mostly — and old movies."

"Journalism, then. Do you like writing?"

"Some," I say, not wanting to tell him about my writing book.

He takes another piece of candy. "Tell you what," he says, "I'll send down to the record office for your transcript and see if I can figure out the new computer long enough to punch out the names of some colleges that have strong journalism departments. Are you interested?"

"Well, I guess there's no harm in getting some information," I say. Mr. Harris is so sincere, I don't have the heart to tell him that I probably won't be going to college at all, that I'm just wasting his time.

"No harm at all," he says, reaching for some papers behind him. "For now, why don't you fill out this preliminary work sheet? Also, I'll need an autobiography. You can use this guide sheet to see what to write. Oh, and one more thing. It might be a good idea to take the SATs this weekend."

He hands me all the papers. "The SATs? I didn't even know they were being given," I say. "Don't you have to send away an application to take the test?"

"Ordinarily yes," he says, "but you can just appear at the test this Saturday with this form I'll give you and you can be a walk-in candidate, okay?"

"Do I have to take it?" I ask.

"Well, it can't hurt, and in your case I'd strongly recommend it. Your average isn't all that high and I think the SATs will help you. Why don't you try it? Then we'll have a lot more to go on. If it doesn't work out, it doesn't work out. You can always go to the community college around here."

He smiles. I know he's trying to help, but all these tests and forms are getting me confused. I said I would go to the interview, not sign up for a mess of exams.

Mr. Harris asks me what's wrong. "I'm not sure I want to go to college," I blurt out. "I don't know what courses to take or anything. Aren't you supposed to have it all figured out before you enter college?"

"Who told you that?" he says, taking another piece of candy. "If students knew exactly what they wanted, I'd be out of a job. Most kids, I've found, need a small push. Tell you what. Let's get the ball rolling on these forms and see what happens. I can't tell you how to handle your life, but I think I can provide a few options for you. Fair enough?"

"Yeah, that sounds okay," I say. I feel slightly uncomfortable because I'm not going to do anything with these forms anyway.

"We still have plenty of work to do with you, though," he says, getting up. "But I have the feeling that once you know what is out there, some answers will become clear to you. Who knows, maybe I'll see you on TV one day — Richie Linder, NBC News."

The man is a mind reader.

"Listen," he says, "come back next week, same time, same station, and I'll let you know what I have for you.

And don't forget about the SATs. Do you want me to call your – "

"Richie, Richie, hurry, I've been looking all over for you. I have to talk to you," Lana says, bursting into the office and coming to a sliding stop in front of Mr. Harris's desk. "Oh, excuse me," she says to him, "I didn't mean to interrupt."

Mr. Harris looks at her and says, "Catch your breath, young lady. Is there an emergency?"

Lana turns to me and says, "Richie, come to room 215 as soon as you can. I'll go save a place for you."

"A place for what?" I ask.

"You'll see, just hurry!" she says as she dashes out of the office.

"Who was that?" Mr. Harris asks, looking surprised.

"A friend of mine," I say.

"Is she always like that?"

"Yeah."

"Okay, I'll let you go. We're almost finished anyway. I was about to say, Do you want me to speak to your father and tell him the arrangements we made?"

"No, no, I'll speak to him."

"Fine. See you next week then. Better go see what your friend wants."

I'm heading for room 215 when I run into Eric and Venezia. "Hey, what's the rush?" he says. "Aren't you going to history?"

"No, I've got something to do," I say.

"That figures," he says. "I just saw your friend Lana

and she said if I saw you to tell you to hurry up. Go ahead, convince me there's nothing going on between you two."

"There's nothing going on," I say. "We're just friends, that's all." I really don't need Eric interrogating me.

"Biologically impossible," Eric says, smiling at Venezia, who doesn't say anything but smiles back at him. Does she ever say anything? She's certainly different from Lana, that's for sure.

"I gotta go," I say to Eric. "See ya."

"See ya," he says, walking off hand in hand with Venezia.

As I walk quickly to room 215, I get the feeling that I won't be seeing much of Eric from now on. Sure, we're in the same classes, but it's not the same thing. He's so wrapped up in Venezia, there's no time for anything else. We used to talk a lot together.

The sign outside of room 215 reads:

Limited number of staff positions available
Join *The Record*, if you're good enough
Become active in high school journalism

Meeting today
Room 215
1 p.m.
Be on time
First ten applicants to appear
Will be tested today

The notice is signed G. Treadwell.

"Lana, you creep," I murmur to myself. "What are you getting me into?"

I knock on the door and enter a fair-sized room where fifteen or so people are clinging to several pieces of furniture. I hold on to the inside doorknob.

"Yes?" says Treadwell, standing there in his impeccable three-piece suit. He's holding a pair of glasses in his hand. He looks like some professional, a doctor or lawyer maybe, not a teacher.

"I'm looking for someone," I say.

"Don't hedge, young man," he says in a rich, deep voice that sounds like a TV anchorman. "Good journalism requires a commitment. Either you're inside or out." I let go of the door handle.

I can see why people are scared of him. That voice could intimidate anyone.

I see Lana in the corner of the room. "Here, take my number," she says.

"What's this?" I ask, looking at the 7 printed on an index card.

"Just take the number," she says. "I gotta split. See you later."

"Lana, wait!" I say, but she's already at the door. Treadwell stops her and says in that commanding voice of his, "Where are you going, miss?"

"Oh, I'm in the wrong room," she says sweetly. "I thought this was the tryouts for cheerleaders. Ta-ta." She's out of the door before Treadwell has a chance to say anything.

Treadwell looks over the room, waits for total silence,

and after a dramatic pause begins, "I suppose all of you who were lucky enough to get numbers today to apply for staff positions think you will become famous journalists. I want to disabuse you of that idea right away. Journalism is a jungle; I know because I spent ten years out in the real world of deadlines and by-lines. It's a shrinking jungle too. Newspapers fold every day. So if you're foolhardy enough to try it anyway, you might as well be prepared and serious about it. I'm tough, but good, and after a year with me you'll know the basics. With a little hard work you might even become competent journalists."

He sounds charming, I think, but somehow I'm intrigued.

"The school paper," he continues, "has won more prizes than any other paper in the state. And do you know why? Because I run the paper my way. What I say goes. I know this is supposed to be the age of 'do your own thing' and 'free expression,' but if you want to come out of this year thinking like a journalist, you'll have to learn how to obey orders — mine."

His voice resonates across the room. Orders. Sounds familiar, I think.

"Now we come to a little exercise in deadline journalism," he says. "Each of you with a number will now be given the opportunity to prove your journalistic mettle under actual newsroom conditions. Keep the story straight and factual. Emphasis is always on the facts. Today I would like a news story about the new dietitian in the school. The facts are printed on this rexo. Harding, will you please hand out these papers."

I turn to see a clone of Treadwell. Harding is a tall, skinny kid also dressed in a three-piece suit.

"Harding is my managing editor," Treadwell explains. "He will watch you. I will return in exactly one half hour, by which time you will have committed to paper a news story commensurate with your skill and intelligence. Remember, stick to the facts."

I look over the rexo; it's just a bunch of notes about recipes, prices and deliveries — nothing interesting.

I think for a few minutes and then begin to write, slowly at first and then with more confidence. It's like I'm writing in my notebook. The words come easily. Some of what I write actually makes me smile.

I still have time to proofread the piece before Treadwell sweeps into the room and says, "Who wants to be first?"

No one stirs.

"I'm disappointed," Treadwell says. "Journalists have to be aggressive. Number seven, let's start with you."

I look at my index card. Number 7 all right. I hand him my story, and he puts on his glasses and begins to read:

> To say that the food in the cafeteria is unappetizing would be to compliment it too highly. The mashed potatoes look like brothers of the Blob and the beans are so old they're has-beens.
>
> We're mad and we're not going to take it anymore.
>
> Gruel would be a step up in cuisine. The frankfurters walk under their own power and the fries are week- (or weak) old rejects from Burger King.

Here is a proposal: Have the United Nations send *us* CARE packages. If that doesn't work, remove all the food from the cafeteria and have the help there feed us intravenously.

We're mad and we're not going to take it anymore.

The bread can be used for penicillin, the hamburgers for Frisbees, and the spaghetti for live bait.

Students, unite. You have nothing to lose but your stomachs.

"You write this?" Treadwell asks, putting his glasses back in his pocket and looking straight through me. The expression on his face is definitely not friendly.

"Yes, sir," I say.

"Are you a comedian?"

"Huh?" I say, surprised.

"Or a wise guy?" His face is inches away from me, his voice low and steady.

"I don't understand," I say, stepping backward.

"Then let me enlighten you," he says. "If I tell you what to write, give you the outline to follow, I certainly don't expect you to go off on a malicious tangent. What kind of news story is this?"

"Well, it's not a news story directly." I stammer, trying to figure out what to say. "Just my feelings about the cafeteria, that's all. I thought I would try a little humor. The topic seemed so dry."

"You thought? How nice," he says in a low voice edged with ice. "Who told you to think? All I wanted you to do was to follow the facts of the story, not create your own fairy tale. A newspaper is based on facts, young man, not fanciful fiction. I will not have my journalists concocting sophomoric satires just to satisfy their notions of adolescent humor."

What's he talking about? I think, getting angry. I turn to go. Lana and her big ideas.

"You have a lot to learn about writing, young man, but I'm afraid with your attitude there's nothing much I can teach you."

"What attitude? You're the one with the attitude," I answer back.

"Watch what you say," he says threateningly, still speaking in that low voice. "Did you come here just to cause trouble? And where is that girl you replaced? Don't think I didn't see that little switch of numbers. Did she put you up to this? I want to speak to her."

I don't say anything. This makes Treadwell even more upset. He twirls his glasses. "I want her name," he says evenly.

No way, I think. Why should Lana get in trouble for something I wrote?

"I'd like your name and hers," Treadwell says. He goes over to his desk and pulls out a piece of paper. "You can write it on this."

I think of Lana and what she tried to do for me. Angry now, I shout out, "You can take this paper and shove it!"

"What did you say?" Treadwell says, turning around.

"You heard me," I say, making a quick move for the door and slamming it on my way out.

What a jerk I am, I think outside in the hall. Treadwell

will probably boil me in oil if he gets his hands on me. I don't care. I said what I had to say. I don't care what he thinks. What does he know anyway? Just how to boss people. I can write; I'll show them all.

I'm thinking all this as I walk back home to the luncheonette. Who wants to join that stupid paper anyway? All I want to do is go upstairs, watch television, and shut out the whole world. I'm halfway in the door when my father stops me.

"How did it go?" he asks.

"How did what go?"

"The interview. You went, didn't you?"

"Yeah."

"And?"

"And all right. The college guy wasn't too bad. He gave me a lot of forms to fill out."

"What did he say?"

"I'm scholarship material."

"Get serious."

"I'm telling you. He gave me these forms and said I should take the SATs this weekend."

"I want you to go upstairs and study," he says firmly.

"What? Are you kidding? Study for what?" I ask.

"I don't kid about your future. The SATs are very important. I want you to go up to your room and hit those books now."

"But, Dad, there's nothing to study," I say. I don't believe he's for real. Studying? It's the last thing I want to do.

"There's always something to study," my father says,

getting a mean look in his eyes. "You're not weaseling out of this one. Do you hear me? You're grounded until those exams. I'll handle the store myself. Get up to your room and – "

"Hi, Richie. Told you I'd drop by. Like the jacket? It's my mother's. She has dozens of them."

Lana gives me a smile, turns and aims the same smile at my father. "Hi, you must be Mr. Linder. Pleased to meet you. Richie has told me all about you," she says, taking my father's hand.

"Who's this?" my father says, turning to me while shaking Lana's hand.

"Dad, this is Lana Olivia Turner, from school."

"How do you do," he says slowly. I can see my father doesn't know quite what to say. "You'll excuse me, miss, I've got some customers to attend to. Pleased to meet you too. Richie, don't take too long. You've got things to do."

"So that's the ogre," Lana says when my father is out of earshot. "I expected something different – like Godzilla."

"Sssh, he'll hear you," I say. "That was some trick you pulled on me in the newspaper office, leaving me like that."

"How did it work out?" Lana asks.

"It didn't," I say. "He threw me out for something I wrote. He didn't appreciate what I said about the cafeteria. I still think he's gonna come after me."

"See how your writing moves people?" she quips.

"Very funny."

"Well, don't let it get you down," she says, hopping on a counter stool. "Treadwell seemed a bit difficult. I guess he just doesn't recognize star quality in the making. At least you tried."

"A bit difficult? The man's crazy," I say, joining her on the next stool. "You want something to drink?"

"No thanks. Hey, forget about Treadwell. There'll be other challenges. What sign are you? Aquarius?"

"No, Taurus. Why?" I ask.

"That doesn't surprise me. As I said, you're a bull."

"You said I was a rock."

"Rock, bull, what's the difference? They're both tough." she laughs.

"Anyway, I appreciate you trying to get me on the paper," I say. "It was a nice thing to do."

"Hey, what are friends for?" she says.

Lana looks around the store. "Oh boy, you've got Body Count. I love it."

"You've heard of it?" I ask.

"Are you for real? Of course I've heard of it. I own the record — 3,147 kills with one quarter. I'm so good it's boring already. I think I'll take a crack at the other one."

She calls out to my father, who's at the end of the counter. "Oh, Mr. Linder, do you have change of a dollar? I want to play the baseball game."

"On me, miss, if you're Richie's friend," my father calls back. He slides a quarter the length of the counter. Lana fields it expertly. "Hit the red button for the starting lineups."

"Are the batting averages this year, or are they life-time?" Lana asks when the machine lights up.

"I never bothered to ask," my father asks, surprised.

"I was just curious," Lana says, inserting the coin into the machine. "Oh, and does this game vary the pitching speeds? I hate hitting just fastballs — too easy."

"I think it has curves and change-ups," my father says, staring at Lana. I can tell he doesn't know what to make of her. Neither do I.

"Oh, super! Batter up, then," Lana says as the lights on the machine begin to dance and the first few bars of the national anthem are played.

My father moves closer to me. "Is she in your class?" he asks.

"Sort of," I say.

"She's not a beauty, but a nice kid, lively, you know what I mean?"

"Yes."

"Are you and she — "

"No, Dad, please, we're just friends, that's all."

"Oh," he says, looking somewhat disappointed.

Someone calls out for a hamburger and my father goes to put one on the grill. I walk over to Lana. She's already on her thirty-fifth run in the first inning. "The game's a snap," she says. I watch the little men run the bases.

"Well, did I pass inspection?" she whispers.

"You're sneaky, you know that?"

"What did I do?" she says innocently.

"I bet you went to charm school too. 'Pleased to meet you.'" I mimic.

"He's very nice, Linder. Not the monster you painted."

"I didn't say he was a monster, only difficult."

"Well, he's not Frankenstein," Lana says, continuing to belt out base hits. "Actually, he cares about you, I can tell."

"How?"

"The way he looks at you and then me. I bet he thinks we're an item. What did you tell him?" she asks.

"Nothing. I just said that we were friends."

"Right. Friends. Listen, are we okay for this weekend? Can you be ready at four A.M.? I'll pick you up."

"On what — a bicycle?"

"Never you mind. You just be ready," she says, turning around. "Oh, damn, you made me mess up my timing." Her game ends. "Four A.M., remember."

"I don't know," I say.

"Richie, I'm counting on you. It's no fun camping alone. How about that Coke now? That game made me thirsty."

I get her the Coke, which she drinks in one swallow. "Listen, I have to run now. You want to walk me?" she says.

My father hears the last part of this and says, "Sorry, miss, he can't go anywhere now. He has some very important work to do."

Lana shrugs her shoulders and walks out the door.

I look at my father in amazement. Again telling me what to do. And when to do it. No way. No more. I run out of the door and catch up to Lana. "I'll be ready," I say. "Just don't ring the bell."

"Super," she says, "we'll have a great time, you watch."

"Richie, get the hell back in here," I hear my father yelling.

"Yes, Dad, right away," I say.

I watch Lana walking down the street, her red, fuzzy hair blowing in the wind. We are friends. Right.

Chapter 8

FOUR A.M. I'M WAITING outside the store for Lana. It is still dark and there is no sign of her. Maybe she won't show; maybe she forgot. I don't feel sleepy at all, just a bit jumpy. I did leave my father a note telling him I'm going camping with a friend. Still, I'm nervous.

I walk a few steps to the corner to where a street light shines dully. I park myself on a hydrant and wait. To get the thought of my father out of my head I take out my writing notebook. My mind is clear, like that of a fugitive on the run, even though I couldn't fall asleep last night and watched a late movie on TV. An idea just pours out of me onto the paper:

> Good morning, Mr. Linder. This is a picture of Miss Lana Olivia Turner. In her checkered career she has assumed many disguises. The second picture you

hold shows her wearing a fur jacket and impersonating a movie star. In her life she has posed as a lumberjack, model, and tennis star. We do not know what her next disguise will be, but be careful. She is on a special mission to liberate a young galley slave from the clutches of an old luncheonette owner and show him there is life beyond high school, college, and SAT exams. Her latest caper involves rescuing said galley slave and spiriting him off to the woods. Your mission, should you accept it, is to enjoy your freedom and not worry about a thing. As usual, Richie, should you be captured by any large, cigar-smoking foreign agent, the secretary will disavow any knowledge of your action. This notebook will self-destruct in five seconds.

I look up and down the street. No Lana. I don't think she's coming. This is a crazy idea anyway. I start walking back to the luncheonette.

A jeep screeches to a stop in front of me. Lana, or somebody resembling Lana, climbs out. "Lana, what did you do to yourself?" I ask. I hardly recognize her. Her red hair is straightened, pulled back into two tight pigtails. She is wearing a peasant blouse, green camping shorts with matching suspenders, white knee-length athletic socks, and expensive tan hiking boots.

"I love to go a-wanderin'," she says. "Climb in."

"Where did you get the jeep?"

"How dare you call it a jeep?" she says, ignoring my question. "I'll have you know that this is a Land Rover, the aristocrat of off-the-road exploring."

"Where'd you get it?"

"From a friend of mine, runs a garage over on Eighteenth. He owes me a favor, so here it is."

"What's that on top?" I ask, pointing to a large carton that is strapped to the roof.

"A surprise," she says.

"I don't like surprises."

"You'll like this one. Come on, already. I've got the map, the lantern, everything."

"Your mother knows you're taking all this stuff?" I ask.

"What are you—the FBI? Of course she knows. She told me to have a good time. She's overjoyed that I'm doing something healthy for a change. Are you ready to go or what?"

"Let's hit the road," I say as I slide into the seat next to her.

In spite of its weird appearance, the Land Rover is quite comfortable. I'm amazed how skillful Lana is with a stick shift. "Learned in Florida on a dune buggy," she explains. "My father showed me how to drive. I think he wanted to race cars once."

"This is the life," I say, settling back in my seat.

"We haven't done anything yet," she says. "Here, hold these maps. We may need them and then again we may not."

I crane my neck toward the back of the Rover and see a whole lot of equipment. "Are you sure you brought enough?" I ask.

"Probably not," she says.

"Did you bring a radio?"

"Oh, good Lord," she says slamming the wheel with her hand. "Listen to me, sweety, we are leaving civilization far behind, hear me? Far behind. No radios, no TV, no nothing. We'll talk. That's what they used to do in the good old days."

I look at the map for a second. "What do you want to talk about?" I say. "Did you see the late movie on channel seven last night?"

"Richie!" she screams in mock horror. "Why is everything with you TV? Ever notice that?"

I look at the map again. "Lana," I say, "this is a Florida state map."

She takes the map and quickly looks at it. "Whoops," she says, "wrong map. I think we're gonna have to wing it."

"You don't know where you're going?"

"Sure, I know where we're going. Besides, I've got the instincts of a homing pigeon, pal, don't worry. I heard about this great place. Just look for some landmarks. We'll play it by ear."

"What landmarks?"

"Richie, if you're going to be a famous writer you'll have to take risks, go against the tide."

"Not knowing where I'm going upsets me," I say.

"Look at it as a metaphor for life. Who needs a map anyway? I have a compass. As long as we're heading north, we're okay."

"I don't know," I say.

"Trust me," Lana says. "Pretend we're on an exotic safari."

"Like they have in *National Geographic*? I used to love that magazine. Read it all the time."

"Secondhand living," Lana says sharply.

"Why are you always putting me down just because I haven't done or seen the things you have?"

"Because in your polite pseudo-humble way you feel sorry for yourself, and if there's one thing I can't stand it's self-pity."

"You're beginning to sound a lot like my father."

"Well, maybe he's not totally wrong about you."

We drive around a while in silence. The scenery is still pretty boring, nothing but gas tanks and factories. If this is the wide open spaces it smells, literally. The sky, though, is not boring. Fingers of orange light begin to scratch the sky. It's quiet too, except for the whine of our tires and an occasional car that swooshes by us in the opposite direction.

The factories and their smells give way in time to other signs: Al's Garage, Sleepytime Mattress Company, Second Methodist Church. "Still no country," I say to Lana. "Are you sure we're headed in the right direction?"

"I'll honk when I see a cow," Lana says. "And I'm sorry about that crack about your father. I really don't know him."

"No, you don't," I say. "He works me to death."

"You call that work? It must be fun making sodas all day."

"Of course, it's work. I've been in that store every day since I was ten years old, even before that."

"If you don't want to work, don't. That simple."

I look out the window. We're on the highway now. Still no cows. "The work I can deal with," I say. "What I can't deal with is my father. He's always there, always around. My shadow."

Lana looks over at me and says, "I envy you. At least you have your father around. I miss mine."

I'm surprised anyone could be jealous of my father.

"How's your friend, Eric?" Lana asks.

"All right, I guess. I don't see him much. Maybe he's planning on eloping with Venezia."

"I don't believe in love," Lana says, which surprises me because she's always talking about feelings and emotions.

"Why not?" I ask.

"Because life's too short to tie yourself down to one thing or one person. Keep movin'. That's my personal motto. That way you can't get trapped. Did I ever tell you I had a job once—as a checker in a supermarket. Talk about being trapped."

"But you don't have to work," I say. "Your folks have money."

"Just the point. I don't have to work, but I had to prove something to my mother. She made me feel like a freeloader or something, a flower child born twenty years too late, she called it. Hey, keep your eyes on the road. Tell me when we hit Route 80. You name the statistic and I'm part of the survey. If my mother reads that seventy-five percent of teenagers try drugs, she figures I'm running a dope ring. If ten percent are involved with crime, I'm responsible for five percent. She's absolutely convinced that if she doesn't watch me like a hawk I'll be public enemy number one."

"What was the job like?"

"Pure torture. You want to hear how I got fired? Of course you do. This lady gets on my line and accuses me of tasting her yogurt. 'Lady, I didn't touch your yogurt,' I say. 'You did,' she screams and calls the manager. I freaked. They had to hold me back from dumping the yogurt on her head. The manager comes over and fires me – fires me! Something about making a scene. I can still see my mother smiling and thinking, See fool, I knew you couldn't hold down a job. My therapist heard about this for months. Any sign of Route 80?"

"No," I say.

We settle into a driving routine over the next hour. I look out the window, for cows maybe, and Lana sings, a bit off key.

There are more cars on the road now, not a whole lot more, but several bearing license plates of different states. I remember that when I was a kid there was a certain kind of cereal I liked because it had miniature license plates in the box and over a period of time I collected the whole set, except for Utah. I could never get Utah. I liked the exotic-sounding names of places I did get, like Idaho and Wyoming, Wisconsin and Minnesota. They could have been foreign countries for all I knew. What were the people living there like? Do they have luncheonettes in Kansas?

"Hey, there's the turnoff up ahead for 80," I say.

"I see it," Lana says. "Get ready for a banked right turn."

"Lana, did you ever fly a plane?" I ask.

"Don't ask silly questions. Do you remember the old Jefferson Airplane?" Lana says, as she makes the turn onto Route 80.

"Is it in the Smithsonian Museum?" I say.

"Hey, that's not half bad. I do believe you're developing a sense of humor."

Route 80 is a two-lane highway with trees alongside casting morning shadows across the blacktop. The road is cracked, so occasionally we hit a bump that lifts us out of our seats. "Ever read *The Grapes of Wrath*?" I ask Lana.

After a half hour of bouncing around Lana turns off 80. Two small towns and a dirt road later she pulls the Land Rover into a wooded grove. "End of the line," she says. "Help me unpack."

"Where are we?" I say.

"Home, home on the range," she says, stretching her arms out. "Let's get a move on; we have to set up camp."

"Are there any bears around?"

"Only lions and tigers. Let's go."

I feel like Gunga Din, a great movie by the way. In addition to the backpack Lana straps on me, I carry in one free hand a rolled-up tent with poles inside, and in the other hand the kerosene lamp, fishing rods, and assorted junk.

"Hey, how come I'm doing all the heavy work?" I say.

"Because I'm carrying this!" Lana says, hoisting to her shoulders the large carton that was atop the Land Rover.

"Still not going to tell me what's in the box?"

"Nope. Let's move out. It's only a mile hike to the campsite," Lana says. "We just follow the river."

"Call car service," I say.

I have to admit the area is very beautiful. Trees protect us from the sun as we walk along the little trail that parallels the river. It's already early afternoon.

"Who painted red circles on the trees?" I ask.

"They're trail markers, in case you get lost."

"I thought people use bread crumbs."

"Oh, give me a break, will ya," she says, smiling.

Eventually the trail opens up to a grassy patch of land. "You put up the tent and I'll look for firewood," Lana says.

A manual would help, as I try to make sense of the stakes, ropes, and ground cloth scattered at my feet. I put up one center pole; the other one collapses. A locking device closes on my finger.

"Howya comin'?" Lana asks, returning with her arms full of wood.

"Where'd you put the instructions? Even Tinker Toys come with a set of instructions."

"Watch," she says. "Nothing to it." She has the tent up in two minutes. She must have been raised by the Indians.

"Lana, wait a sec," I say, looking around on the ground. "Didn't we forget something?"

"I brought everything we need," she says, stacking the wood in a neat pile.

"Food, Lana, food."

"I didn't bring much, just some gorp, you know, some survival food. That and a few bags of potato chips. It's in my knapsack."

"You didn't bring anything else?"

"I have a bottle of wine with me. I think it'll go nicely with fish, don't you?"

"Where are we going to fish?" I ask, surrendering.

"From that rock over there," Lana says, pointing to a spot some fifty yards away. "But first we gotta find some worms."

"Yuck," I say.

"The classic American experience, Richie. Huck Finn time. C'mon, a worm ain't gonna kill you. I'll even hook it on the line for you. I swear, didn't your father ever take you fishing?"

"He just cooks them; he doesn't catch them."

Lana starts looking around for worms. "Richie, there are serious gaps in your education. You are culturally disadvantaged. Do you know that? You'll write about this one day, I know it."

A few minutes later I'm standing on a rock, dangling a line in the water and drowning a worm. "Sssh," says Lana. "You have to be very quiet. I think I see some fish."

This is not too bad, I decide. I could get used to this kind of life. The air is sweet and pleasant, and I like the way the breeze runs through the trees. Lana studies the water. It's peaceful here, like a still-life photograph — the sun, the water, Lana, all caught in a freeze frame. Best of all, there is no one yelling at me, no one telling me what to do. Right now I should be in some stupid classroom sweating over some dumb SAT questions. This is the better life, much better. I think I could stay here forever.

We spend a good part of the afternoon fishing. I don't catch anything, but Lana does. "Let's save these for supper," she says, holding up her fish. "I've brought some Granola bars too. They're around here someplace. It'll keep away the munchies."

The afternoon slips into evening. We go for a little walk around the campsite. Lana knows the name of various trees and flowers. It's like a crash course in botany. I'm very happy; I wish I never had to go back to face the world, school — and my father.

Later, by the light of the fire and the kerosene lamp, and filled with the fish Lana had caught and I had pan-fried (seems I can never get away from cooking), I pour some wine into two paper cups. Lana sits next to me, her face aglow. I hold the cup of wine up to the sky and start singing, way off key.

"You're feeling good," Lana says softly. "Must be the wine. Go easy on it. I only brought one bottle."

"We will drink no wine before its time," I say. "Quick, it's time. Pour more wine."

"Yes, sir," Lana says, "anything else?"

"Now that you mention it," I say, putting my arm around her. The wine is making me feel very good.

"What's this for?" she says, looking at me strangely.

"For all this," I say, waving at the sky.

"I didn't do much. This is all free scenery."

"You helped," I say. "I never would have done this on my own. I'm glad you're here." I can feel my face getting warmer.

"And I'm glad you're here," she says quickly. "Now that that's all settled, let's clean up this mess. Big plans for tomorrow. I got a few surprises that will knock your socks off."

I pull Lana closer to me.

"Hey, pal, what are you doing?"

"Nothing. I just thought I'd move a bit closer. You know, the stars, the wine, you." I tighten my arm around her waist.

"Are you getting romantic ideas?" she asks. Her voice is guarded, definitely not romantic .

"Could be," I say.

"I think the wine has gone to your head."

"You've gone to my head," I say suddenly. I didn't even think about saying that. It just came out.

"Oh, Richie, you're sweet, but that's a bad line, even for television." I take my hand off her waist and stare into the fire. "Oh, c'mon, you're too sensitive," she says. "You know I like you."

"Thanks a lot."

"Richie, you're very nice."

"Then sit closer to me."

She touches my arm. "You sure you want to change the rules?" she says.

"What rules?"

"I don't know if we should get into something heavy," she says. "It'll change us."

"How do you mean?"

Lana pokes the fire with a stick. Then she says, "What we have is very special, very comfortable. Don't spoil it."

"What are you talking about?" I say, beginning to get upset. "I thought we could be close. Is that so awful?"

"It's not awful, just not right for us."

"Not right?"

"No, it's not. A physical relationship is always so — well, intense. It burns out quickly. I don't know if we're ready for that kind of relationship. I've had some pretty lousy relationships in the past and I don't want to louse this one up by rushing into anything."

I get up and walk around. I feel too angry to say anything. Picking up some pieces of wood and throwing them in the fire, I realize I don't understand her at all.

Lana, still sitting, turns her face toward me and says, "Richie, please. I was afraid you might misunderstand my feelings for you. Listen, what we have is a good friendship, one of my all-time best. Can't we leave it at that? You know I care for you very much."

"Oh sure," I say, still pretty upset. The wine — or is it Lana? — is beginning to give me a huge headache.

"It's true, Richie, you know it's true. Also, I don't

want you to get the wrong impression about me. I don't sleep around, although my therapist says I could be more selective."

"You talk to your therapist about sex?"

"Of course I do," Lana says, with a forced little laugh. "Don't be so naive. I still have to discover my sexual identity."

"I'll help you," I say.

"You're making this more difficult than it has to be," she says. "I need our friendship much more than a quick squeeze. I need to know that you like me as a friend. And I know you do. Don't change that. I feel normal and good when I'm with you."

"Great, just great," I say sourly. The pounding in my head is increasing.

"Richie," she says in a voice both sad and pleading, "I'm afraid of being alone, afraid of cracking up. You see how people at school look at me. I can't help the way I am. My mother thinks I'm this close to going over the edge."

"Are you?"

"No, not now. Not when I'm with you. I've moved around so much I feel like I'm an ad for a Rand McNally map. I need friends right now, good friends, not lovers. And I need you."

She bites her lower lip and doesn't say anything more. I think I see tears in her eyes, but I don't know what to say. I'm hurt, more than a bit angry, but at the same time I feel sorry for her. "Lana," I say finally, "you confuse me. You say you like me, but you push me away.

I think you just pretend at getting close to people, but you really keep everybody away. It's a great act."

Lana flinches, but says nothing. She takes a small piece of wood and balances it on her finger. I've hurt her, but I didn't mean to. Silence stands like a wall between us. Should I apologize? Should I hold her hand? Or should I just shake her? My feelings are all mixed up.

She takes a deep breath and says softly, "Maybe we should talk about something else, okay?"

"I'm feeling kind of tired," I say, "and my head hurts — the wine, I guess."

"Okay, then," Lana says. "Maybe we better just turn in, separate sleeping bags, of course." She tries to smile.

"All right," I say. I don't feel as good as I did before. But I'd still rather be here with Lana than in the city. She is a puzzle — I'll never figure her out. Why is everything with people so complicated?

Chapter 9

I FEEL A NUDGE on my shoulder. "Linder," Lana whispers, "how do you feel about a rafting expedition?"

"I want to sleep," I mumble, trying to crawl deeper into my sleeping bag. My head still hurts. "What are you talking about? We don't have a raft. Go back to sleep."

"Rise and shine, Richie, and greet the new day," she says. "We're going to conquer this mighty river, come hell or high water."

"Have you flipped?" I say, sitting up. "This is a small stream."

Lana pulls out a map from her shirt pocket. "Found it last night stuffed in my sleeping bag. Knew I had it. According to my calculations, this stream, as you call it, opens up to a lake. Look, see here, the trail that we were on yesterday continues and parallels the river."

I take the map from her. The river opens up all right. I look at Lana to see if she's serious. "Why don't we just take the trail?" I ask.

"Did you ever see the movie *The African Queen*?" she says. "I'm sure you did — you've seen every movie ever made. Well, I'm Rose and you're Charlie."

"Lana, get serious," I say, crawling out of my sleeping bag. "We're in the middle of nowhere. There's no place to rent a boat."

"True, but wait till you see what I have." She gets up, goes over to the big carton she carried the other day. "*Voilà*," she says.

"Tell me you've got a boat in there," I say.

"Nope, not a real boat. Actually it's a raft, our very own *African Queen*. She opens up the carton. Inside is a deflated rubber raft. She pulls two cords — *whoosh!* — and the raft inflates like a balloon. "It's navy surplus," Lana explains. "Did I tell you my father was in the navy?"

"Unreal. You are definitely unbelievable," I say.

"I know," she says, smiling. She seems to be her old self again.

"About last night," I say. "Maybe we should talk."

"What's to talk about?" she says, smoothing out the wrinkles in the raft. "Last night was last night. This is a whole new glorious day. Maybe we should christen this thing."

"We don't have any champagne. We drank all the wine last night, remember?"

"No matter," she says. "What would you like to call it?"

"*HMS Titanic,*" I offer.

"Very funny," she says. "Let's call it the *African Queen*. I've always loved that movie."

We carry the raft to the water's edge and put it in. I'm surprised how light it is. Lana jumps in and stumbles a bit, almost tipping the raft over. "Careful," I say. "You have to move slowly in a small boat."

"Aye, aye, captain," she says. "And for breakfast *du jour* we have two bags of potato chips," she adds. "Here, catch."

With two small paddles we make our way down-stream — or is it upstream? I'm not sure. Lana sits in front of me. I try to catch the rhythm of her paddling. "Small boat sets sail out of the harbor after all," I say softly to myself thinking of the dream I had.

"Did you say something?" Lana asks.

"Nothing, it's nothing, just a thought I had."

"Well, keep paddling, partner. I want to find the lake," she says.

"Lana, this is crazy," I say over her shoulder. I can just see the papers now: Rescuers today found the bodies of two teenagers who attempted to find a nonexistent lake. Funeral services for the pair will be held tomorrow.

"That's what's wrong with you, Richie," Lana says, purposely splashing water on me. "No sense of adventure. You want everything safe and guaranteed. Well, I don't want to live my life like that. And I don't want you to live like that either. You've got to take some risks with people."

"See what happened when I tried — last night?"

"I'm not talking about that. That was something else entirely. We're both not ready for that."

"What do you want me to do?" I say.

"Just live — live and write about that."

"My life isn't so interesting," I say.

"So write about mine," Lana says. "Tell you what — you play reporter and I'll be the person you interview. Got your pad? No? Just fire some questions at me any-way — go ahead."

"Like what?"

"You're the reporter. Make like Mike Wallace."

"I don't know what to ask. Let's see. . . . What do you think about school?"

"You're unreal!" she says, splashing me again. "That's a dumb question. You've got to gain my confidence, not depress me. School? They teach you what you don't need to know — all facts, no feeling. Ask me another question."

"How do you feel about the world situation?"

"How the hell should I know? There's not a whole lot I can do about it. Richie, you've got to come up with better questions. This is boring, bor-ing!"

"There is something I've wanted to know. You're always talking about your father. If he's so great, how come you're not living with him?"

She turns around, stops paddling.

"Be careful," I say.

"Yeah, yeah. No sweat." Then she looks directly at me and says, "Hmm, that's definitely a better question. Just because you love a person doesn't mean he loves you back, that you can live with him. You know that crap how all relationships should be fifty–fifty? That's bull. It's more like seventy-five–twenty-five, never equal."

"Lana, you don't have to – " I start to say.

"Sometimes," Lana says, going right on, "I feel I always give more than I get back. With my father it was a funny thing. When I was a kid and we were all living together, one big happy family – at least most of the time – it was great. Then, I don't know, he sort of lost interest in me, didn't want to do things with me. Had other things on his mind, I guess. I mean, he's a great guy and all, but it's like he didn't know what to do with me when I hit thirteen. I stopped being his girl and started to fight with both him and my mother, about everything. He couldn't handle it and spent more and more time out of the house, messing around. Finally, Split City. I suppose if I had kept my mouth shut my parents would still be together. I don't know."

She catches her breath; her face looks upset, twisted with sharp lines. "Look, maybe this is none of my business," I say. "Maybe we should – "

"Of course it's your business," she cuts me off. "Who else am I gonna talk to? C'mon, a follow-up question. Don't get cold feet. I'm all right, really I am."

We have stopped paddling and are just drifting toward

some dead branches in the water. It is very quiet. I can hear the crickets chattering on the shore. "What did you do that was so terrible?" I ask, feeling like I'm trespassing, but curious nonetheless.

"Nothing really," she sighs, gazing for a moment out over the water. She rubs her eyes for a second, turns back toward me and continues. "I ran away a couple of times to sort things out. I'd hitch a few rides and when I'd finally get tired of all the running, I'd phone my parents from some small jerkwater town in the sticks and they would pick me up. I can remember all the rides home. They would speak to me like I was an egg or something ready to crack—you know, that deliberately soft voice guaranteed not to cause additional trauma. Things would be calm for a while, but I would hear them arguing into the night, each blaming the other for why I was such a screwup. I don't think my father wanted to fight all the time. He just wanted to be left alone. So after a while, when the fighting just got worse, my mother did just that—left him alone. That's how we came here. You want to hear something else? The bottom-line truth? Neither of them really wanted me. My mother got me by default. I thought my father would stand up to my mother and say, 'I want her,' but he didn't. All he said at the airport was, 'It's best you go with your mother.' They didn't even love me enough to fight over me."

Lana starts to cry. Tears stream down her face. I don't know what to say—I've never seen her this upset before.

"See what you started?" she says, wiping her face with her arm. "Oh, Richie, don't look so grief-stricken. I'm okay. I didn't mean to lay this all on you, really I didn't, but it gets to me sometimes. Hey, forget about it. Let's get back to some serious paddling. I want to see that lake."

"You sure you're all right?" I say, touching her arm.

"Sure, sure," she says. "Let's move on. We didn't come all this way just to hang around. Do you remember the name of the river they went down in *The African Queen*?"

"I don't," I say watching her.

"Hey, captain," Lana says a few minutes later, as we continue to paddle, occasionally skirting a few rocks jutting up from the water. "Ain't this the great life? Nobody around, so-o-o peaceful. How do you feel about God, Richie?"

"What kind of question is that?"

"Do you believe there is a God or not? Simple question."

"I guess so. Doesn't everyone believe in God?" I say hesitantly. Lana's questions from left field continue to surprise me.

"You think he's everywhere, watching everybody and all?"

"Sure. Why not? If he's God he can do anything he wants."

"Well, I don't see it that way at all," she says. "Oh, I believe there is a God and all that, but I think he's pretty selective about the places he takes care of. Take this river, for example. I bet it's one of his pet projects. Everything's in place here. I think he's pretty much given up on cities. Whenever he gets sick and tired of the mess people have made of this planet he throws down another Ice Age or flood and starts all over again."

"Like the story of Noah and the flood," I say.

"Exactly. I have no doubts that that particular Sunday school story is a hundred percent true. I just hope he waits a few years before he starts housecleaning again."

"I never thought about it that way," I say. "I thought God was supposed to be perfect."

"I'm sure he is," Lana says, "but what he made sure isn't. People fighting all the time and not just in families. But do you want to know something? I think God is an eternal optimist. Look, if he can admit mistakes and start all over again, anybody can, including me."

"And here I thought you were perfect."

"You did? That's sweet. But really, despite what my parents think, I'm just like every one else, just as scared. Only I hide it better, that's all. Most of the time I'm a very good actress, in case you hadn't noticed."

"That's for sure. You could be a profess——" I start to say.

"Remember when you said by the campfire that I pretend at getting close to people," she says, cutting me off, "and I push them away? That bothered me a whole lot, but you know, you're right. You hit the nail on the head."

"I still like you, actress or not."

"I know that you do. That means a lot to me, Richie. You know you're much nicer than I am. You don't go around hurting people. I could learn something from you."

"Rose and Charlie, Charlie and Rose," I say. "Think we should make a movie about all this?"

"No way," Lana says. "This is a private friendship, just between us. That's why I like it. Listen, how about you rowing for a while? I'm a bit bushed. All this fresh air is making me drowsy. I leave the bridge of this ship in your capable hands, captain. Wake me up if you see the lake."

Lana rests her head on the inside edge of the raft and in a few moments is fast asleep. I look at her curled up like a kitten. Even in her sleep she can't stay still, I think, as she squirms to find a more comfortable spot in the front part of the raft. I paddle slowly in the center of the river, which now seems to be widening, maneuvering the raft as carefully as I can because I don't want anything to jar or upset her. I feel I never want to upset her — now or in the future. What was she saying about relationships? Seventy-five–twenty-five? Well, I know what I've given and it's not all that much. Look at all she's done for me — her encouragement, her support, this trip — and she doesn't ask anything more from me than my being there. Someone's on my side now. I realize this, bobbing in a small rubber boat in the middle of a river.

Even though Lana can obviously take care of herself, I feel I want to protect her, make up for all the rotten things that have happened in her life. Why? I don't know. I do know she makes me feel that I am a better person than I am. Seeing her sleeping there, I realize that I love Lana. I want to wake her up and hug her, keep her with me as we hop in the Land Rover and travel cross-country together. I have this feeling that with Lana there's nothing I couldn't do, absolutely nothing.

Lana is still asleep as I guide the raft around a bend in the river and suddenly come upon the lake. It's incredibly beautiful. Sunlight makes speckled dots shimmer on the water, and huge trees line the shore on all sides. The lake is smaller than I thought it would be, more like a pond.

I paddle out to the center of the lake, a hundred yards or so offshore, because I want Lana to see it all at once. I wish I could give her the lake as a present.

"Lana, wake up, we're here," I say, touching her shoulder.

"Where's the lake?" she mumbles sleepily.

"We're on it," I say.

"Super," she says. Then, without thinking, Lana suddenly stands up in the raft. "Richie, it's gorge——"

"Lana, sit down. La——"

But it's too late. Very quickly, the raft flips over. I fall overboard to one side; Lana falls the other way.

"Lana!" I scream when I bob back up to the surface I don't see her. "Lana!" The raft floats between us.

"Richie, help, I can't swim. Richie!"

"Where are you? I can't see you."

"Other side. I'm holding on to the raft. It's sinking — it must have caught on something. Hurry!"

I swim as fast as I can to the other side of the raft and see Lana holding on. "I can't make it, Richie. Please!"

I grab hold of her with one arm and with the other I hang on to the raft. I hear a slow, hissing sound — air escaping.

"Richie, I can't hold on. Shit. What a lousy way to die. The *Titanic* is right."

"You're not going to die," I say. "Can you float on your back?"

"Barely."

"Well, try it. Hang on to me. Don't worry, I'll get you to shore."

"Richie, the raft's going down."

"I got you now. Easy does it."

Struggling, I swim with one hand and pull Lana with the other.

"This is stupid, we'll never make it," Lana says as some water washes over her face.

"Shup up and just relax," I say. "Quit talking for once and try not to swallow so much water. Just breathe through your nose. We'll make it."

"Aye, aye, captain," she says, choking on more water.

I am not sure we will make it, though. Even though Lana is buoyed up somewhat by the water, she feels very heavy. Those damn boots. I feel the edges of panic in my stomach. Think about something else. I force myself to think of all those laps I used to do at the "Y" pool and try to calculate the distances I covered. I get a picture, momentarily, of my mother and the way she taught me to swim. My mother's dead. Quit it. Think of something else. What a good story this would be to write about, if I — change that, we — live to tell about it.

The shore grows closer. I look at Lana, who is trying to help by stroking with her arms. Just a few more yards. C'mon, I tell myself, you can do it. I'm cold, tired, and aching — push it. Just a few more yards — please, God.

"Richie, I can't," Lana says.

"Yes, you can — we're almost there."

Using the very last of my strength, I finally reach a large branch sticking out from the shore and with a lunge pull myself and Lana onto the bank. We both collapse on solid ground.

For a few moments the only sound I hear is Lana coughing and crickets all around us. I lie stretched out on the ground, thinking we both could have died and nobody would have known.

Lana sits up; she looks a mess. I can't tell whether she's laughing or crying as she tries to catch her breath.

"Well . . . I . . . promised . . . you . . . an . . . adventure," she sputters.

"You're crazy," I say. "Why didn't you tell me you couldn't swim?"

"You didn't ask me that question in the interview, remember?"

"Don't make jokes. We both could have drowned out there, you know that?"

Lana looks over the water. There is no sign of anything, not even the raft. "Yeah, I know that," she says. She wipes her face with her arm. "Richie, I had faith in you," she says, shivering. After a few seconds she adds, "I knew you wouldn't let me go, ever. Sorry I screwed up. Par for the course."

"How do you feel?" I ask.

"Okay, I guess. I don't think I'll ever be dry or warm again. What about you?"

"I'm all right," I say.

"All right? Richie, you were fantastic. Where the hell did you learn to swim like that? I mean, that's right out of the movies. Hey, do you realize we followed the script?"

"What script?" I say, trying to wring out my shirt, which is plastered against me.

"*The African Queen*," she says. "Don't you remember? The boat sinks and Rose and Charlie are the only two survivors. Tell me you don't remember that."

Lana gets up slowly. "Listen," she says, "I don't want to embarrass you or anything, but do you realize what you did? You saved my stupid life, you know that? Anybody else would have just thought of his own skin, but you didn't. Superman to the rescue. You're absolutely the greatest person in the world. Stand up. I want to give you the squishiest hug and kiss of all time."

"Does this mean our relationship is changing?" I say, taking her into my arms.

"Boy, are you slow," she says. "It already has. Hold me, Richie. I'm still shaking, for God's sake. Hold me tight...."

Chapter 10

"I'M STARVED," I say later to Lana. "We haven't eaten anything all day, except those potato chips."

"I guess we should be getting back," she says flatly. "It's gonna be a long walk. Maybe we can find some berries on the trail."

I'm feeling so good that berries sound like a feast. "I haven't thought about getting back at all," I say. "Wouldn't it be great if we could just stay here?"

"That would be great," Lana says without enthusiasm.

What's with her? A few minutes ago she was lively and bubbly; now she seems someplace else. "Are you okay?" I ask.

"Sure, just tired, that's all," she says. But I have the feeling it's more than that. Well, I'm not going to let her change of mood determine how I feel. I want to feel this confident forever.

"Ah-choo!" she sneezes.

Clouds darken the sky as we head back on the trail that parallels the river. Lana doesn't say much except "look out for that branch" or "that rock" as she quickly moves through the trees. She does find some berries and we eat them on the way. I want to say something to pick up her spirits, but what? I have this sinking feeling that the good times are over. It's funny that almost drowning can be considered a "good time," but it was, a definite thumbs-up experience.

We get back to the campsite and load up the Land Rover just before the rain begins, introducing itself with a light shower that gradually builds up to a steady downpour. We quickly pack the Land Rover and start back toward Route 80. The windshield wipers slap back and forth as we ride to the city, mostly in silence. Lana looks straight ahead while driving, not saying anything. She sneezes a lot, but she doesn't say anything. It's like I'm not there.

The trip home is long and boring. Lana hardly says two words the whole way. It's dark by the time she stops the Land Rover in front of the luncheonette and turns off the motor. "I'm beat," I say. "I just want to crawl into bed and sleep for years. I may skip school tomorrow. What about you?"

Lana doesn't hear me; she looks exhausted. She slumps her head on the steering wheel. "Hey, Lana," I say. "You okay? I thought we had a good time out there, except for the small fact we nearly drowned."

She doesn't even smile.

"Lana, what gives? You're always telling me not to sit on my feelings, and you're the one who clams up. I don't get it."

"Listen, I gotta go," she says, turning on the motor and sneezing again. The Land Rover sputters to life. It seems exhausted too.

"Hold on a sec," I say, reaching over and taking the key out of the ignition. "What's going on here? Are you mad at me?"

"I don't feel like talking just now," she says.

"When, then?"

"Later, after I have a chance to sort things out. This was one heavy weekend, you might have noticed."

"Why are you being so mysterious? Let's talk."

"Not now. Don't ask me any more questions."

"Okay. I'll call you later then."

"No, don't do that. I'll call you when I'm ready."

"Ready for what?" I say, getting angry. "Come off it. I have one of the best times in my whole life with someone I happen to care about, maybe even love, and now because a mood hits her, she ignores me. Can you tell me what the hell is going on? You know I love you." I'm shouting the last words.

"I know that you do," she says quietly. "That's part of the problem."

"Problem? What problem?" I feel totally confused.

"Look, I can't explain it to you now," she says, starting up the Rover again. "I can't even explain it to myself.

Just give me some room, okay?" She tries a small smile that comes out lopsided.

"You're not mad at me?"

"Mad at you? Where'd you get that idea? Richie, you're the greatest, the best, don't you forget it. It's my problem." She gives me a quick kiss good-bye, puts the Land Rover in gear and drives away.

As the taillights disappear around the corner, I suddenly think about my father. It's the first time I've thought of him in a long while.

The lights are still on in the luncheonette. I peek in the window. I know what's coming, but I don't have the strength to face my father now. All I want to do is sleep.

Fortunately, Ernie is working alone behind the register. I know how much my father hates to pay overtime. I walk in quietly and sit on a counter stool. The store is empty.

"Oh, you're back," Ernie says. The man must be great at telling stories.

"Where's my father?"

"I wouldn't be in such a rush to see him."

"Is he angry?" I say, looking around the store.

"You better avoid him," Ernie says.

"Thanks for the warning."

I tiptoe up the stairs but have no luck, because there at the top of the landing stands my father, waiting. I don't like the look on his face.

"Hi, Dad," I say. "Listen, I know you're — "

He smacks me hard across the face when I get into range. "What did you do that for?" I yell, stepping backwards.

He advances toward me again. By reflex I put up my hands to ward off any more blows. Instead he shouts, "You stupid idiot! What are you trying to do, kill me? Where do you come off running away like that without telling me nothing?" His arms wave an inch in front of my face. Is he going to hit me again?

"I left you a note," I try to say.

"What good's a stupid note? What the hell are you using for brains these days? I turn my back for a second and you take off for God knows where. Just because your friend Eric's crazy, you gotta be crazy too?"

I don't say anything about Lana; somehow I feel it would make matters worse.

"What are you so angry for?" I say.

"Your test. You missed your test."

"It's just one SAT, for crying out loud. I can take it again, later."

"Where? When?" he snaps.

"I don't know."

"What do you know? You know how to give me a heart attack. That's what you know."

Suddenly the weekend with Lana seems very far away. "I just needed to get away, that's all."

"Oh, excuse me, your royal highness," he says savagely. "You have it so rough, don't you. Who are you trying to kid? You have a little exam, not very important.

it just decides your whole future, and you run away from it like a scared rabbit. You're nothing but a baby, you've always been a baby."

"Dad, that's not fair."

"Don't talk to me about what's fair. It's fair of you to mess up your life, to do anything you damn please? I don't work all day in this store so you can run around the country like some delinquent."

Another round and I'm getting killed. "What do you want from me?" I scream back at him. "Leave me alone!"

"What do I want from you?" he says mocking me. "That's good, that's really good. Grow up, for God's sake. You're seventeen — you do absolutely nothing to help yourself or anybody else, for that matter."

"I saved somebody's life this weekend."

"What the hell are you talking about? What kind of idiotic stories are you making up now?"

"Never mind — you wouldn't understand."

"I don't know what to do with you anymore," he says. "Everybody's got a son to be proud of. What have I got? A spineless jellyfish who runs away and thinks only of his own pleasures."

"It's not that way at all," I say. "You've got it all wrong."

"I'm ashamed of you, you hear me, ashamed of you. I'm almost glad your mother, God rest her soul, isn't here to see this."

Something snaps inside of me and without thinking I punch him hard in the stomach, his fat, greasy stomach.

He doubles over, holds his stomach, and then roars, "Get out of here, you bum. I don't want to see your face — ever!"

I run down the steps and out of the luncheonette. I don't know where to go, what to do. I'm scared like I've never been before, worse than on the lake. Lana! I gotta call her. At a pay phone on the corner I quickly find her number through the operator and dial. The phone rings and rings. Lana, please be home.

"Hello," a voice says.

"Hello, Lana?"

"This is the answering service."

"Is Lana there?"

"This is the answering service. Do you wish to leave a message?"

"Can I please speak to Lana? It's an emergency."

"The doctor is not in, sir. Do you wish to leave a message?" The voice by now grows icy.

"No message," I say.

"Thank you for calling," the voice says.

As I hang up the phone, it occurs to me that I can't get through to anyone. What am I going to do now?

"Hello, Eric."

"Linder, what the hell are you doing here this time of night, man? God, you look a mess. Where were you?"

"You wouldn't believe me if I told you. Can I come in?"

"Isn't it bad enough I have to see your ugly face during the day?" he says.

153

"No jokes, please. My father just threw me out of the house."

"Permanently?"

"I don't know, I don't think so, who knows. Can I stay over? Would your parents mind?"

"Do you see my parents? They're away on a weekend, went off to some motel like a couple of kids. Embarrassing, man. Something about a marriage encounter group — you know, renewing their vows and that sort of crap."

I walk inside and flop down on the couch in the living room. "What happened to the great romantic?" I say. "The last time I saw you, you were practically walking down the aisle with Venezia. By the way, where is she?"

"I don't want to talk about it, man," he says, sitting down next to me.

"That's okay. I don't feel much like talking either. Can I sleep on this?" I say, patting the soft pillows of the sofa.

"She dumped me," Eric says with a deep sigh.

"When did all this happen?" I ask.

"Yesterday. Her father set her up with the son of an army buddy of his, some hotshot cadet up at West Point, home on leave or something."

"I thought her old man liked you."

"So did I. But he messed me up good. It's all a matter of stripes anyway." He sees the quizzical look on my face. "You don't understand what I'm talking about, do you?"

"Nope," I say, leaning back on the sofa. My whole body aches.

"West Point beats the military college I'm going to, so I guess her old man looks into the future and decides he'd rather have a West Point man for a son-in-law. It's simple — I just got outranked."

"Why did she go out with him when she's going out with you — to make you jealous?"

"Man, you know nothing about women, do you?" he says, beginning to get angry. I think of Lana and silently agree. "Of course she wanted to make me jealous. I find the girl of my dreams, treat her like a princess, and then she turns around and stabs me with a saber. I wish I had that West Point guy between the cross hairs of an M-16."

"Maybe she doesn't like this guy," I say, trying to calm him down.

"And maybe she does," Eric says loudly. "Man, you can't trust girls for nothing."

I really don't need to be more depressed. "Listen," I say, "do you have anything to eat? I'm starved."

"Oh yeah, sure, man. Help yourself to anything in the fridge. My parents left enough food for an army."

I head for the kitchen, look in the refrigerator and pull out some cake and milk.

"I wonder if I can join the French foreign legion," Eric calls from the other room.

"You don't even speak French," I say, my mouth full of cake. "You're letting a girl do that to you?"

He walks into the kitchen and pours himself some milk. "What are you looking at me like that for?" he says. "I'm not crazy; you're the crazy one. You have a little argument with your father and you make like it's World War III."

"It was. I hit him."

"You hit him? Oh, wow, man, you didn't tell me that. Did you hurt him?"

"I don't think so. Kind of surprised him. Surprised me too," I say.

"You goin' back? I mean, I can't put you up for weeks."

"Just for tonight, Eric. I gotta figure out what to do. I need some time to think."

"Sure, man. Take all the time you want. I'm goin' upstairs and write Venezia a letter telling her what I really think of the way she acted. You want to help me write it? You're much better in English than I am."

"Naah, you go ahead. I just want to sit here for a while."

Eric goes upstairs and I just sit with my cake and milk. I can hear the kitchen clock ticking. I put my hand on the telephone that sits on a counter near me. Should I call him? What can I say? Something like, "Hey, Dad, sorry I belted you," or "Hey, Dad, I'm not sorry I belted you. Don't come near me, I might hit you again."

I feel awful — sorry and not sorry at the same time.

And what about Lana? Should I try to call her up again? Maybe she'll pick up the phone this time. I gotta get some sleep now; maybe I'll be able to think more clearly tomorrow.

Eric and I walk to school the next day. "Hey, do you ever see that weird girl around?" he asks referring to Lana.

"Some," I say. If I told him about Lana I'd never hear the end of it. "Finish your letter?" I ask.

"Sure, man, it's a beaut," he says, pushing the hair out of his eyes. "You know, something hit me last night while I was writing it. Why the hell am I giving up? I mean, if a general has a military setback, does he fold his tent and run away? No way, man. He regroups his forces and charges back up the hill."

"You're going to storm her house?" I ask.

"I tried to write her the nastiest letter I could, but the words didn't come, man. I kept picturing her beautiful body in my mind. I wound up writing her a love letter. You want to hear it?"

"No, I don't think so," I say.

"Trouble with you, Linder, is that you have no heart," he says. "You need a transplant."

We walk past the old "Y" building. What if I just go swimming, I think.

"You think I'll get Venezia back?" Eric asks.

"How would I know?" I say testily. "I'm no Dear Abby. I don't have a heart, remember?"

It's still a few minutes before the first period and the halls are crowded. Eric goes off to find Venezia and

I walk into Gortkin's math class. I feel like I don't belong there.

Gortkin enters precisely as the late bell rings, and announces, "I haven't been happy with the homework I've seen, or to put it another way, the homework I haven't seen. So, scholars, we are going to have a little surprise quiz." Groans fill the room. "There are ten problems on these papers I'm handing out," he says. "Please do your best to supply the answers and keep your eyes on your own paper."

I stare at the sheet in front of me. I can't figure out how to do one problem, let alone ten. After fifteen minutes all I see on my paper is a doodled red balloon rising over a lake.

The rest of the morning is not much better. Mrs. Fabrikant discusses a chapter from *The Grapes of Wrath* I haven't read. I don't even have my books with me. Patterson marks me down for being unprepared in gym, and Ms. Poquette, lovely, radiant Ms. Poquette, ignores me completely.

What a wasted day. There is a pounding in my brain that is getting louder. I want to see Lana; I've got to see her. Is she in school? I doubt it, I would have seen her by now. Maybe I should go over to her house.

Out of habit I start walking to the library, when Eric practically jumps on my back. He's grinning idiotically. "You'll never guess what happened, man, it's the greatest," he shouts. He's jumping all around. People are looking at him.

"What are you hollering about?" I ask.

"Venezia, of course. She's back, back in my arms again. She read my letter and positively flipped."

The only time I've seen Eric this excited is when he's drooling over some new weapon system or when he met Venezia in the first place.

"We took a nice long walk together just before," he says, his eyes dancing. "She said she was bored silly by that upperclassman and couldn't wait to see me again. Said she went out with him because her father forced her to. You might be the best man at my wedding sooner than you think, buddy boy, dress uniforms all the way. Catch you later — I gotta go meet her now. You okay?"

He doesn't wait for an answer, but races down the hall.

No, I'm not okay. Everything's screwed up. I feel totally miserable. Where are all the good feelings I had about myself? Sunk with the *African Queen*. Why did I hit him? I wonder if I should call my father and get this whole mess resolved one way or another. I should never have come back from the camping trip. Never. Maybe I'm just crazy. High school, college, my love life, just down the tubes. I gotta call my father. He'll kill me, but I've gotta call.

What if I write down carefully what I'd say to him? If I'm forceful enough, if I stand up to him, maybe he'll listen to my side of the story. Where's my writing notebook? Home — no good. I'll get some looseleaf paper from Mrs. Resnick.

But instead of writing about what I could say to my father, I find myself drawing pictures of the lake and writing about Lana, the trip, the accident, and most of all my feelings for her, in the poem she wanted. I write for about a half hour, I think.

"Hey, pal, gone swimming lately?"

Lana!

I jump up and hug her. The librarian gives me a look and then moves away.

"Easy, Superman," she says, "don't get too close. I have a cold you would not believe and a touch of fever — must have caught it in the tropics." She looks horribly wonderful. Her skin is all pasty, except for her nose, which looks like a bright red Christmas light that sort of matches her red hair.

"Lana, it's great to see you," I say.

"Look, I can't stay very long. My mother would have a fit if she knew I skipped. Rest — that's what the doctor ordered. I knew you'd be here, Richie. You're still a creature of habit. I just had to see you, just had to."

"I wasn't sure you'd want to see me again," I say. "Not after the trip home. I tried to call you, but all I got was the answering service."

"I was in no condition to speak to anyone. Man, was I out of it. Delirious City. But it was a fantastic trip, wasn't it?"

"Fantastic? What about the trip back?"

"Hold on — ah-choo! I'll explain in a second. Anyway, I come home and have this humongous fight with my mother. It was a classic. Remember when I told you that I had my mother's blessing to go? Well, that's stretching it. To be honest, I lied. She didn't know where

I was. She hit the roof, positively went through it, calling me every name in the book, beginning with 'thoughtless' and ending with 'irresponsible.' My mother may be right. I don't even have a driver's license. Ah-choo!"

"Are you kidding?" I say. "We could have been picked up by the police."

"I like living dangerously," she says simply. "Anyway, she accused me of every imaginable crime. One funny line, though. She asked why couldn't I go to a motel like other normal teenagers. I told her the weekend was a natural, breathtaking high, and she wanted to know the name of the pervert who dragged me off to the woods. I didn't tell her the boat sank; she would have positively freaked. And I didn't reveal your true identity, Superman, don't worry."

"I don't care about that, Lana," I say. "I'm just happy to see you."

"Which brings me to my real reason — ah-choo! — for coming here. You might have noticed that I acted more weird than my usual weird self on the homeward voyage, double bubonic plague notwithstanding; but as I said in the Rover, I had things to work out — things between us."

"What things?" I ask, afraid for a second to look at her directly.

"You know me," she says. "I have a little trouble with relationships, not only with adults, but with people I like — no, love — like you, Richie." I look up.

"Don't act so surprised, will ya," she continues. "This is hard enough for me to say." She takes out her big red bandanna and blows her nose. "It wasn't just our communal dip in the lake or the time afterward, it was everything. You've always been wonderful to me, Richie, more than a friend, but I'm afraid. Commitment is not my strong suit; you may have noticed that too, but I feel committed to you, Superman. And as long as I'm sitting here laying my heart out on the table and junk, I might as well tell you that all that business about me and other guys — well, that was an exaggeration too. I never felt as close with anyone as I felt with you after the raft turned over. It was wonderful."

"All that stuff about your old boyfriends was made up?"

"I told you I was a good actress."

"But why?"

"I'm more afraid than you are."

"That's hard to believe."

"Believe it — no games, Richie. I'm being straight with you. What we have here is your basic heavy relationship. It feels good, feels right, and I want it to continue. No promises either, just me in living color. Only let's go slowly with this thing, okay? Maybe I'll always be a runner, I don't know, but I want to stop spinning my wheels for a while. Slowly, okay? Do we have a deal? Say, what are you doing next weekend? Want to go camping again? Richie, I love you," she shouts out loud. The librarian turns around again.

"I know you do," I say quietly.

"Enough of this mush. I gotta get back. My mother's probably sent out a posse by now. Say, what's this?" Lana says, picking up my paper from the table.

"Just some things I've written about us."

"Can I read it?" she asks.

"Take it with you," I say. "I kind of like the poem."

"Richie, the writer," she says. "It's got a classy ring to it. See you later. I'll call you when the heat's off, I promise. *Ciao,* my changed relationship, love ya, keep writing."

In all of this, I realize after she hurries out of the library door, I didn't tell her anything about my father and me. Maybe it's better. It's something I have to handle myself.

Chapter 11

I DECIDE ON A PLAN. I'll call up the luncheonette and if Ernie's there I'll ask him what kind of mood my father's in. But what if my father picks up the phone and says he never wants to see me again? I have to talk to him. I can't leave things this way.

Why not? A small voice enters my mind. Isn't this what you wanted—a clean break, hit the road Jack, don't you come back no more, no more?

I can't do that. I have to leave on my own terms, not his. How many times can I run away?

Walking downstairs I think I see Eric and Venezia strolling hand in hand. Well, that's all right, perfectly all right. Maybe we can all double soon, to an air show even. Lana would get along with Eric, I'm sure of it.

At the phone in the lobby I reach in my pocket for a dime and dial home.

"Linder's Luncheonette."

Thank God, Ernie. "It's me, Ernie," I say.

"Richie, where are you?"

"At school. I slept over at a friend's house. My father around?"

"I'll get him." Ernie says.

"No, wait. Is he angry?"

"What do you think? Of course he is. When you coming home?"

"In a little bit. Maybe. I don't know, Ernie. Maybe I shouldn't."

"Well, if you ask me you better. I've never seen him so mad. He's been growling at the customers something fierce all morning. What did you do to him? It must have been pretty bad."

I certainly don't feel like telling Ernie the whole story. "Just tell him I'm okay," I say. "I'll get in touch with him."

"When?"

"I don't know."

"Okay, it's your funeral," Ernie says.

The phone clicks and I'm standing there with the receiver in my hand, not moving, knowing what I have to do; knowing, too, what I'm afraid to do. Funeral is right. I feel my stomach tying itself in knots.

"Are you planning to take the phone with you? I'd like to make a call if you've finished."

I turn around and see Mr. Harris, the college counselor. He's fumbling around for some change.

"Oh, Richie, how are you doing? How was the SAT?" he says, dropping a coin in the slot.

"I blew it, the SAT exam," I say kind of softly.

"Stupid phone in my office doesn't work. Must be all that installation of new equipment. How did you do on the SAT? I didn't hear you."

"I didn't take the exam," I say.

He hangs up the phone, collects his dime, and studies me for a second. "Is that why you're looking like your life is over?" he says, smiling.

"It may be over shortly. Want to come to my funeral?" I say weakly.

He adjusts the glasses on his nose. "I think we better have a talk, Richie. Why don't you come up to my office and we'll kick it around."

"What about your call?"

"It can wait. No emergency. Come on, we can't discuss such important matters as your funeral standing here in the hall, can we? Do you think I should wear my black suit?"

"What for?"

"Your funeral," he says, chuckling.

I follow him upstairs to his office, which still has the nice musty smell I remember.

"So what's up?" he says, settling into his chair.

"I told you. I messed up. I didn't take the exam."

"Any reason?" he says, reaching over to the jar of candy on his desk and popping a sour ball into his mouth.

"I went camping with a friend."

"That's not a capital offense. Hardly a reason for planning your final sendoff. Did you have a good time?"

"It was great. I wish I was still up there." With Lana, I add to myself.

"Maybe you'll be a forest ranger," he says. I know he's trying to be nice, but I don't see anything funny in all of this.

"Okay, okay," he says. "I assure you, there's still plenty of time to take the SATs and go to college, if that's what you really want."

"I don't know," I say, staring at the floor.

"Something else going on?" he asks suddenly.

"Huh?"

"Richie, I've been a counselor a good long time and nobody, but nobody gets as upset as you look over a missed SAT. You want to tell me about it?"

"I . . . can handle it," I say.

"You sure?"

"Yeah. . . . No, not really. My father . . . he . . . he threw me out of the house yesterday. I can't go home."

"Of course you can," Mr. Harris says with that same smile. "You can always go home. That's why they call it 'home.' Let me get this straight. You missed your exam and he throws you out? That right?" I'm beginning to hate that smile of his.

"You don't understand. . . . I hit him!" I practically shout out. "I punched my own father."

Mr. Harris takes off his glasses and twirls them for a second. "That must have hurt both of you. No wonder you're upset," he says after a pause.

I can't say anything, I feel so choked up.

Mr. Harris puts on his glasses again. "I could see what the computers have on foster homes," he says. I look at him in amazement. He's making jokes!

"You know, Richie, you're lucky," he says. "Your father's interested in you. He —"

"How can you say that?"

"Let me finish. He's interested in you, in your well-being. All right, he might not be able to express it in the right way, but I'm sure he cares about you."

"But I hit him. I hit him. He doesn't want me."

"I'm sure you don't beat him up regularly, do you? And are you quite sure he doesn't want you? Everybody fights with their parents — well, maybe not so literally. It comes with the territory."

"I hit him, don't you understand that?"

"Sure I understand. But I also understand that he wants to be a part of your life, perhaps too much so. Don't shut him out. You still need him and he still needs you."

"By the way," Mr. Harris says after a few seconds, "where is your mother in all of this? You never mention her."

"She died a couple of years ago."

"Oh, I'm sorry, I didn't know that," he says. "It must be very rough on your father."

I thought he was going to say, "rough on you." Then he says, "You must miss her too."

"I try not to think about it," I say, thinking about it.

"He's got a hard job being both mother and father to you."

168

"He never talks about it, her death I mean."

"Neither do you," Mr. Harris says, looking straight at me.

I turn my eyes toward the shelf of college catalogues. If I look at Mr. Harris I know I'm gonna break apart completely and cry. I don't want to do that. "I think I should go home now," I say softly, trying to get a hold of myself.

"Yes, definitely," he says, "and stop putting so much pressure on yourself. Go to the community college, if you like, and take a few courses. I hear they have a weekly newspaper there and even a TV studio. You like journalism, if I remember right."

I think about what Mr. Harris is saying. It makes sense, but I'm not sure. I guess what I want is some iron-clad guarantee that my father won't wipe the floor with me the minute I walk into the luncheonette.

"Okay," I say after a few seconds. "I'll try to talk to him. I guess I was going home anyway, but you helped me make up my mind. I'll let you know how it works out."

"Good," he says. "Drop by and we'll work on your college application together. It's gonna be all right, Richie, count on it." He gets up from behind his desk and reaches out to shake my hand. "It's gonna be fine. Just speak to him," he says.

Walking out of his office I wish I could be as confident as Mr. Harris. What will I say to my father? What will he say to me?

I walk home slowly and pass the old brown "Y"

building again. A swim? It's tempting, but I want to get home and settle this thing once and for all.

I approach the luncheonette with some dread; it's like I'm in an old movie, like I'm James Cagney walking the last mile to the executioner's chair. But maybe I'm Gary Cooper in *High Noon* instead, walking down Main Street to meet my fate. No, check that, make my fate with my father waiting at the end of the street.

Am I exaggerating? Was it always this way between my father and me? To be perfectly honest, I don't think so, not always, not when I was a kid and my mother was still alive. I remember best Saturday mornings — my father joking with the customers downstairs while I watched superheroes protect the world from mean monsters from the warmth of my cozy bed upstairs. "Here comes Mighty Mouse to save the day," followed by Batman, Scooby-Doo, and Yogi Bear. I loved them all. Tom and Jerry, Daffy Duck, and, most of all, the Roadrunner (beep beep). Afterward, I'd come downstairs and my father would make me lunch.

"Can I help you, sir?" my father would say grandly to me, age five.

I'd look at the menu, which I couldn't read yet, and say, "Some Cheerios and a chocolate malted, please."

"That's no lunch, that's not even breakfast," he'd say.

"Please, Dad."

"All right. Yes, sir. Will that be cash or charge?" he'd smile at me.

"Put it on my tab," I'd say.

The line almost always drew a laugh from whatever customers were in the store. While I would eat my Cheerios my father would dance up and down the store, and each time he'd pass me on the way to some customers at the table he'd muss my hair, or tweak my nose, or wipe my face with a napkin. It felt as good as a hug. His smile warmed me. I felt the luncheonette was the center of the universe.

He liked me when I was a kid, most of the time, I think, but as I grew older, and especially after my mother died, I disappointed him. Now, coming back, I must disgust him. *It must be rough on him.* Mr. Harris's words echo in my mind.

The store, once sanctuary years ago, scares me as I'm about to walk in. A line from "Mister Rogers," many years ago, enters my head: "Be brave and then be strong."

There he is—"The Incredible Hulk." I look at him through the store window. He doesn't see me yet. He's turned around, getting a cup of coffee to go. I can tell that's what he is doing by the Styrofoam cup in his hand. How many cups of coffee has he served in his life? How many has he made me serve? The counter stools are filled with customers. I take a deep breath and walk in. Enter the challenger into the ring again.

"Dad, I . . ."

He turns around and stares at me for a second. I clench my fist. Is he gonna hit me?

"Oh, you're back," he says. His tone is flat, noncommittal. I wait for the opening attack. "Put on an apron," he says evenly. "It's murder in here."

Mine, I think. Still nothing. I can't stand it.

"Dad, the apron can wait. We have to talk. I want to —"

"Not now. Can't you see we're busy? Ernie had to leave, his mother again." He draws a cup of coffee. "Nice of you to make an appearance," he adds sarcastically.

First light jabs. Easy to duck.

"Did you eat?" he asks in a flat voice again. What's he up to? I think.

"I'm not hungry," I say slowly, making a conscious effort to keep my voice from cracking.

"See what they want," my father says, pointing to four more customers who have just walked in and have taken the first booth.

"They can wait. Listen, we've —"

"Not now, I said. Later. You hear me? See what they want."

"Hey, bud, you have a menu or something?" one of the four customers says.

My father takes a couple of steps toward me, gives me a hard look, and points to me to give them the menus.

"How about a roast beef on rye with a little Russian dressing on the side," the first customer says after looking at the menu I hand him.

"That sounds like a good idea," says the woman next to him. "Let me have the same." The other couple orders two pastrami sandwiches.

"And four coffees, now, please," the first man says

to me. To his companion he adds, "Stupid team lost again, Sheila. They need a whole new pitching staff."

"Okay, coming up," I say, collecting the menus. "Dad, draw four," I shout over my shoulder.

The next few minutes are so busy that I don't have time to speak to my father at all. I sneak a look at him from time to time, trying to read his face. He seems calm, but so is a boxer poised before he lands the first real blow. To tell the truth, I'm glad for the rush of business, a breathing space before the inevitable confrontation, or final round to come.

How easily I seem to fall into the old pattern: Swiss on rye, hamburger medium, vanilla malted, tuna casserole, new record for Body Count, Bazooka bubble gum, lollipops, and pretzels. My father and I work silently (except for shouting the orders) for a long time, maybe an hour or more, I don't know. As long as we don't talk the time goes by pretty smoothly. There is a rhythm in making sandwiches, getting drinks, and washing glasses, but even though the rhythm is automatic and familiar I can feel the tension of things left unsaid in the pit of my stomach.

"Had enough?" my father says when the rush is over and there are only a couple of people left at the end of the counter.

"Huh?" I say.

"How do you feel?" he asks. Is he concerned or is he just being sarcastic again?

"Exhausted," I say, trying to smile, but he doesn't say anything more and collects the checks from the two last customers. My guard is up, though. The two customers leave and I wait anxiously for the first exchange. I have some trouble breathing normally.

"Dad, say something, will you?" I say finally, now alone in the ring with my father.

"What are you talking about?" he says quietly. I get the feeling of a heavyweight circling the ring.

"Last night," I say. "We have to talk about last night."

"I ain't got nothin' to say. What's done is done." He takes a cloth and begins wiping off the counter.

Oh, no. We are not going to fall into that old pattern again, I think. Silences at twenty paces. "Dad, please. I have to tell you something."

He throws down his rag, wipes his hands on his apron and turns toward me. "What do you want from me?" he says, his voice slowly rising. "I clothe you, feed you, take care of you, and you do *that* to me? To your own father? My own son punches me and now comes crawling back. What do you want me to say? That everything is hunky-dory, right as rain? Are you kidding? Are you nuts?"

"Dad, I'm sorry," I say, not expecting my apology to do any good. "It's just that — "

"The damage is done," he says, cutting me off. "Who needs your apology after what you did? It was a mean, rotten thing to do. It was, it was . . . criminal. Don't expect me to forgive you for that. I can't and I won't."

"I don't expect you to," I say, retreating like a fighter backing into the ropes.

174

"Some son, some gratitude," he says, pressing forward. "Always bailing you out of trouble and this is the thanks I get—a punch in the stomach? That's a good one. I remember once when you were about three you went behind the counter and put your hand on the grill. Who do you suppose picked you up, left everything and ran with you in my arms all the way to the doctor's office?"

"I don't remember that."

"Course you don't, and I suppose you also don't remember all the places I took you to when you were little, like ball games, all the things I bought you, even that TV set in your room. You have a short memory."

I don't say anything.

"You were such an easy kid. It was a pleasure watching you stuff your face with Cheerios. I don't know what happened to you. I know I didn't raise you to be a bum. Only a bum hits his father."

"I said I was sorry."

"Sorry's not good enough," he says, flicking his hand out in disgust. "Go clean up that table."

Someone comes in the store just then and asks for a pack of Newports. While my father gets him the cigarettes, I think I'm losing this round too. Richie Linder, down for the count, a TKO in the last round. Come on, I say to myself, get up off the canvas.

"Go clean up the table," my father says when the customer leaves.

"No," I say, "not until you listen to me."

"Listen to what?" he says. "Your apologies, your excuses?"

"Listen to me. Me, me, me. You never listen to anything I say. You're great at ordering me around. Yeah, you're great at that. You're always on my case, hounding me. Let me lead my own life!"

"Lead your own life. Who the hell is stopping you?"

"You are, you are!" I say, realizing my voice is losing whatever control it had.

"Go find another father, then," he says disgustedly. "I do the best I can." He begins to turn away; he's always turning away.

Not this time, I think. I grab his shoulder. He spins around. "What are you going to do? Hit me again?" he growls. "Just try it and I'll floor you."

"I don't want another father and I don't want to fight," I shout, like a boxer wildly throwing punches but hitting nothing but air. "You want a son to be proud of. I want a father to talk to, not someone who bosses me around all day. Don't turn away. Look at me!" He glares at me, his face red and hard.

"Be proud of me," I say. "Okay, so I don't play baseball and I don't win scholarships like Charlie, but that doesn't mean I'm your slave, a dog to be ordered around. I bet I'm a better swimmer than Charlie," I add crazily.

He looks at me like I've totally flipped out. Maybe I have.

"If you didn't push me so hard, if you weren't on my back all the time," I yell, "this whole stupid thing wouldn't have happened." Control, gain control, I think to myself.

176

"I'm just trying to look out for your best interests," he yells back, "your future. I worry what's gonna happen to you when I'm gone. At night I worry about you."

"Oh, Dad, don't pull that on me, will you. You're gonna be around for years and years. Into the next century. You're as strong as an ox."

"But your future, Richie, your future."

"Leave my future alone, damn it. It'll take care of itself, you just watch. And I'll tell you something else," I say with sudden clarity. "I'm going to college around here, the community college." I'm surprised by the strength of my voice now, but what I say feels right.

This catches him by surprise, like a right hand that has slipped in. "The community college? What kind of future is that?" He's the one back-pedaling now, I feel.

I follow my lead in. "I don't know exactly, but at least it's something. Give me credit for that."

"I want to know which one of your crazy friends put that idea in your head," he counters, the fight still continuing.

"Mr. Harris at the college office. You spoke to him, remember?"

"Strangers you listen to, not your own father."

"I've done nothing but listen to you my whole life, my whole life, every day—work, school friends, everything. You were the one who called Mr. Harris in the first place. I went to please you. I thought you'd be happy I've decided to go to college at all. Thrilled, in fact. I'll be ninety-seven years old before I do anything that pleases you. The hell with this, the hell with your approval. I swear, doesn't anything I do make you happy, anything at all? I'm going upstairs."

"Richie, I—"

"And I want you to know something else. I'm going to college not for you, but for me. Because there are things I have to learn yet, places I want to travel to. Nothing's gonna stop me from . . ."

My father wipes his hand on his apron and awkwardly places it on my shoulder. "Richie," he says, "all I want is the best for—"

"Dad, I didn't mean to hit you," I blurt out suddenly. "I really didn't."

"I know, Richie," he says.

I wait for him to say something more, but he doesn't. His hand still rests on my shoulder. I can feel his touch. There is a softened look in his eyes that suddenly reminds me of the father who would tweak his five-year-old son's nose.

I can feel the tears well up in my eyes. I don't care. I let them run down my face. At that moment I realize that even though I may travel the world, see Eric take over some island in the Pacific and Lana explore mysterious rivers, my father's luncheonette is still in many ways the center of my universe, the touchstone of my existence. And the difficult man who talks all day long to the customers about baseball, I can hate and love at the same time with equal passion, in equal measure.

He takes his hand off my shoulder and looks up. "Listen," he says quietly, "why don't we close up early.

Nothing much doing in the store anyway. To tell you the truth I'm a bit tired. You look tired too. I think I'll go up and lie down for a while. Lock up when you're ready, okay? I want to catch the baseball score on the early news."

"The team lost again," I say.

"You sure?"

"Yeah, I heard it from one of the customers."

"They need some new pitchers."

"Yes," I agree.

"I'm going upstairs," my father says. His eyes sweep around the luncheonette. He takes a rag and wipes a spot off the counter. "Take care of everything," he says as he leaves. I hear his heavy feet on the stairs.

"Will do," I call out. I think he hears me.

The luncheonette seems very quiet now, so quiet I can hear the dull hum of the refrigerator in back. I wipe my face with my sleeve; my eyes feel red. I get a glass of water from the soda fountain, sit heavily on a counter stool near the register, and stare off into space, past the malted-milk machines, past the rack of *TV Guides* and the shelf where the college catalogues are lined up in neat rows.

I sit there for a long time, hearing the sound of my own breathing. Like a fighter after the final bell, I feel tired and drained. I put my head in my arms and rest and think about my father, the luncheonette, and Lana. "It's gonna be all right," I say softly to myself. "Everything's gonna be all right."

I think I hear my father moving around upstairs.

The noise is familiar and comforting. A spot on the counter catches my eye and I wipe it off.

Later, feeling stronger, I get up and take the papers in from outside. The fresh air blows cold against my cheek. It feels good. I look up at the sign, "Linder's Luncheonette" with the final *e* drooping. My sign too, my lighthouse beacon no matter how far I go.

I walk back into the luncheonette, lock the door, and sweep up. Then I turn out the lights and head upstairs.

Contents

Introduction

More than 200 years ago, a group of men met in Philadelphia. This was a very early time in American history. The United States of America was only about ten years old. These men had different ideas and beliefs about the United States and its future. They worked together for many months. The result of their meeting was the United States Constitution.

The United States Constitution is a set of four papers. The words that are written on the papers are very important. Even though the words are more than 200 years old, they still govern us today. The Constitution is the framework of our government.

The original Constitution is kept at the National Archives and Records Administration (NARA) building in Washington, DC. The actual papers are very old, but the public is still allowed to see them. The Constitution is stored inside containers. These containers are made of steel and special glass. Each night the papers are put

This painting by Howard Chandler Christie shows George Washington and others at the second Constitutional Convention in 1787. You can see Washington standing before the room of people, presiding over the convention. Representatives from many states went to Philadelphia for the convention, which lasted from May 25 to September 17, when the Constitution was completed.

into a vault. The vault cannot be broken into or destroyed. This is all done to make sure that the papers will last a long time. Each day the papers are brought out of the vault to be displayed. Many people go to Washington, DC, to see them. The Constitution is an important symbol. It is a symbol of the American way of life. It stands for freedom.

Chapter 1

Charters and Constitutions in Colonial Times

In 1788, the delegates, or representatives, from nine states ratified the Constitution. To ratify means to accept something officially. When the Constitution was ratified, it became an official document of the United States Congress. Congress is a lawmaking group of people. Congress meets to make and change laws.

The United States Congress of today is different from the 1788 Congress. The Congress of today is an American system. The Congress of the late 1700s was modeled after the British government.

During the 1600s and early 1700s, America was not a nation. Much of it was wilderness.

Explorers and traders, from places such as the Netherlands and England, came to America during the 1600s. America had many valuable resources, such as gold, silver, and animal skins. The explorers and traders wanted these resources. They set up trading posts and colonies. Colonies were groups of settlers.

By the mid-1700s, there were thirteen colonies. England controlled the colonies. The colonists followed the laws of the king and queen of England and the English Parliament. Parliament is the group of lawmaking leaders in England.

England could not rule its colonies on a day-to-day basis from across the ocean. England began to use charters. Charters helped England set up local governments in the colonies. Charters were early constitutions. They were legal papers that explained how a local government should work. Also, the charters gave rights to the colonists. For example, the people of each colony were allowed to elect their own representative. A representative is a leader who is chosen to act or speak for many people.

Each colony had its own charter. Charters allowed the colonies to make and maintain local laws. At first, colonists were glad to follow both local and English laws, but the colonists eventually became unhappy with English rule. England began to have problems with the

This scene shows William Penn (1644–1718) receiving the charter for a territory that eventually became the state of Pennsylvania. This document changed hands on March 4, 1681, and named Penn the owner of the territory. The charter was signed by King Charles II of England and was given to Penn as payment for money owed to Penn's father, Sir William Penn.

colonists during the 1760s. Parliament passed special acts, or laws, for the colonists. They passed the Stamp Act in 1765. It placed a tax on paper goods, such as newspapers and playing cards. England would get money for the sale of these goods.

Colonists were unhappy with these taxes. They felt that the Stamp Act and other taxes were not fair. Colonists from Massachusetts planned a meeting with other colonists. Almost all of the colonial leaders came. The meeting was called the Stamp Act Congress. This congress sent a message to England. The congress told Parliament that the colonists would not obey the Stamp Act.

England did not give up on getting money from the colonies. During the next few years, Parliament passed

The Thirteen Colonies

The thirteen colonies are as follows. The years show when the colonies were first settled.

Virginia (1607)
Massachusetts Bay (1620)
New Hampshire (1623)
New York (1624)
Connecticut (1633)
Maryland (1634)
Rhode Island and Providence Plantations (1636)
Delaware (1638)
Pennsylvania (1643)
North Carolina (1653)
New Jersey (1660)
South Carolina (1670)
Georgia (1733)

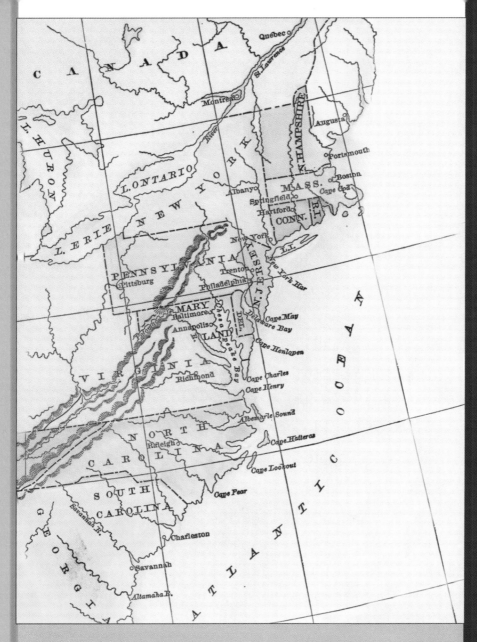

This is a map of the original thirteen colonies. These colonies were ruled by England until 1776, when they broke away and declared themselves free and independent states. They did this by adopting the Declaration of Independence and then using force to gain their independence. This marked the beginning of the United States as a free nation.

more acts. This made the colonists want to unite even more. The colonists formed the Continental Congress in 1774. The Continental Congress was the governing body in America.

Leaders from each colony attended meetings of the Continental Congress. Twelve of the thirteen colonies joined the Continental Congress. Leaders from Georgia did not join right away. Members of Congress spoke to England on behalf of all colonists. England did not want to let go of its ruling power over the colonies. In 1776, Congress decided that it was time to break away from England. Congress told the colonies to make their own constitutions. Each state was told to plan its own government. All English charters were no longer used.

Colonies were allowed to rewrite their own laws without having loyalty to England. Congress declared independence from England on July 4, 1776. They did this through a document called the Declaration of Independence.

Chapter 2

New States in Need of New Rules

Congress made copies of the Declaration of Independence. Copies were sent to all the colonies. By declaring independence, each colony became a free and independent state. Between 1776 and 1777, the states made their own constitutions.

Each state constitution was different. The New Jersey Constitution stated that England was an enemy. The South Carolina Constitution stated that British soldiers robbed and murdered "a number of peaceable, helpless, and unarmed people."

Some constitutions were less angry at England. The first New Hampshire Constitution stated that the colonists hoped an agreement could be reached with England. The Virginia Constitution

began by stating that all men were equal and free. All of the state constitutions helped form the United States Constitution.

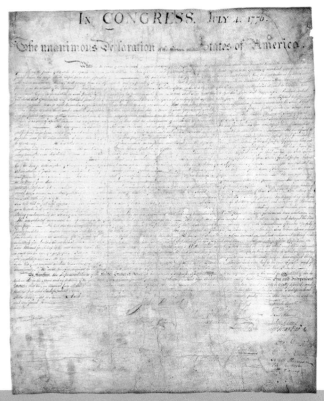

This is a photograph of the original Declaration of Independence. The Declaration of Independence reflects Thomas Jefferson's belief in individual liberty. All fifty-six members of the Continental Congress signed the document, which is now housed in the National Archives and Records Administration building, in Washington, DC.

Richard Henry Lee was very helpful during the colonies' fight for independence. In 1776, Lee declared that the colonies are and ought to be "free and independent states." He also suggested that the states should form a union. His ideas helped form the Articles of Confederation. The Articles of Confederation brought all the states together into one country.

The Delaware Constitution began with the statement that Delaware was no longer a colony and was now a state. New Jersey called itself a colony through its entire constitution. A year later, the constitution was changed. The word "colony" was replaced by the word "state."

The Vermont Constitution declared independence from England. It also declared independence from New York, New Hampshire, and Massachusetts. These colonies had tried to claim Vermont for themselves. Vermont's constitution declared that it would be its own state.

A few of the states gave new purpose to the constitutions. They began to list the rights of people. The Delaware and Vermont Constitutions addressed the issue of slavery. The Vermont Constitution said that no man over the age of twenty-one could be a slave or servant and that no woman over age eighteen could be a slave or servant.

§. 3. 'And whereas laws inconsistent with the spirit of this constitution, or with the public good, may be hastily & unadvisedly passed; be it ordained that the governour for the time being, the Chancellour, & the judges of the supreme court, or any two of them, together with the governour, shall be, & hereby are, constituted a council to revise all bills about to be passed into laws by the legislature: and for that purpose shall assemble themselves, from time to time, when the legislature shall be convened; for which nevertheless, they shall not receive any salary or consideration under any pretence whatever. and that all bills, which have passed the senate and assembly, shall, before they become laws, be presented to the said council for their revisal & consideration; and if upon such revision & consideration it should appear improper to the said council, or a majority of them, that the said bill should become a law of this state, that they return the same, together with their objections thereto in writing to the senate or house of assembly, in whichsoever the same shall have originated who shall enter the objections set down by the council, at large in their minutes, and proceed to reconsider the said bill. but if after such reconsideration two thirds of the said senate or house of assembly, shall, notwithstanding the said objections, agree to pass the same, it shall, together with the objections, be sent to the other branch of the legislature, where it shall also be reconsidered, and if approved by two thirds of the members present, shall be a law. And in order to prevent any unnecessary delays, be it further ordained, That if any bill shall not be returned by the council within ten days after it shall have been presented, the same shall be a law, unless the legislature shall, by their adjournment, render a return of the said bill within ten days impracticable; in which case the bill shall be returned on the first day of the meeting of the legislature, after the expiration of the said ten days.'

41791

Thomas Jefferson is remembered for his writing. These are his notes on the constitution of the state of New York. These notes contain his ideas on how the New York Constitution should be revised. Many of his influential papers, including his draft of the Declaration of Independence, are kept at the Library of Congress, in Washington, DC.

15

The state constitutions listed many rights that were eventually used in the United States Constitution. The New York and Maryland Constitutions said that people had the right to worship in any manner. The Pennsylvania and Vermont Constitutions protected a person's right to say or print anything. Some states protected a person's right to have weapons. These included North Carolina, Pennsylvania, and Vermont. The New York Constitution also protected the Native Americans. It stated that no one was allowed to cheat the Native Americans out of their lands.

Each state also formed its own government. The choice for the type of leader was either a president or a governor. This leader would be elected into office. Most states chose a governor as the leader. Delaware, South Carolina, and Pennsylvania chose a president. Many constitutions also stated that leaders would be elected to attend future Continental Congress meetings.

Most of these new states decided to keep using some English laws. They kept the ones that worked well. Most constitutions also claimed that the state government was not powerful unless the people supported it.

A New Government Chapter 3

The states had their own constitutions and governments by the end of 1777. Members of Congress also felt that all the states should come together to form a union. A union would strengthen the independence of America from other countries. A union would also allow the trade business to work more smoothly.

On November 15, 1777, Congress adopted a document. This document was called the Articles of Confederation. A confederation is a union. This document stated the rules of the union. The name of the union was the United States of America. The states entered into a strong friendship with each other. In times of war with other nations, the states were to come together to protect one another.

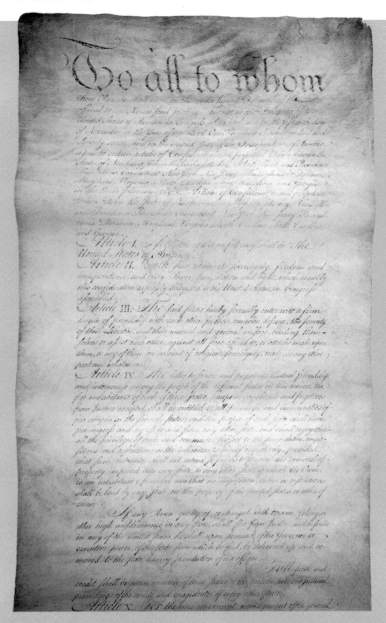

This is a copy of the Articles of Confederation, the document that is considered to be the first constitution of the United States. The Articles of Confederation was only in effect for eight years, and it named the Congress as the governing body of the country. Although it was only in effect for a short time, it is still an important document, as it helped to form the United States Constitution, which is still used today.

The Articles of Confederation was also about the trade business. By trading with one another, the states could get other goods or money. Other countries were also interested in trading with the United States. The Articles of Confederation made it possible for the states to enjoy trade without limits.

The document did have weaknesses. It did not give enough power to Congress. Congress did not have enough power to carry out the rules of the document. Congress could not collect taxes. It could not control the trade business between the states and other countries. Any trade deals that Congress made could be turned down by any of the states. If a state representative did not want to attend Congress meetings, he did not have to.

By 1786, Congress was trying to strengthen its power. A committee decided that the Articles of Confederation needed to be improved. Alexander Hamilton, a representative of New York, invited all state leaders to attend the Constitutional Convention. The Articles of Confederation would be improved and changed at the convention. Each leader could help to change it.

The Constitutional Convention took place in Philadelphia in 1787. It was supposed to begin on May 14, 1787, but it could not officially start until enough leaders arrived. By May 25, enough leaders had come. Rhode Island was the only state that did not send representatives.

The members of the convention decided against making changes to the Articles of the Confederation. There were too many changes to make. The members decided that the United States needed a new type of

Alexander Hamilton, pictured here, is remembered for influencing the United States in many ways during its early years. In addition to being a delegate at the Constitutional Convention, he also served as the United States's first secretary of the treasury and was one of the authors of the Federalist Papers. Many of his ideas and actions helped to shape the United States as we know it today.

government. Instead of revising the Articles of Confederation, they had to make a new document, such as a constitution. This was the beginning of the United States Constitution.

Making a new document and government was not easy. The deputies studied the early state constitutions as well as the Declaration of Independence. Congress hoped that the deputies would create a special government. This government would be balanced. One person or group of people would not have too much power.

George Washington was elected president of the convention. The convention is also known as the Federal Convention and the Grand Convention. It was held at the Philadelphia State

Constitutional Convention Facts

- Members who attended the Constitutional Convention were called deputies.
- The deputies were chosen by their state leaders.
- Deputies came from different backgrounds. They were educators, ministers, doctors, merchants, land owners, investors, and soldiers.
- Forty of the fifty-five deputies were already congressmen in the Continental Congress.
- Benjamin Franklin was the oldest deputy at age eighty-one. Jonathan Dayton was the youngest deputy; he was twenty-six years old.

This illustration ran in a newspaper in 1776. It shows the committee that created the Declaration of Independence. It included (*from left to right*) Benjamin Franklin, Thomas Jefferson, Robert R. Livingston, John Adams, and Roger Sherman. Each of these influential men earned a permanent place in the history of the United States for his work on the Declaration of Independence.

House. This was where the Declaration of Independence was signed. Eight of the deputies who attended the convention had signed the Declaration of Independence. Many great men worked together to make the Constitution. They included Benjamin Franklin and Thomas Jefferson.

We the People Chapter 4

Deputies worked on the United States Constitution throughout the summer of 1787. They discussed many issues. One issue was the amount of power that the government of the United States should have. Another issue was the number of state representatives that should be allowed into the new Congress. Each deputy acted on behalf of his state's concerns. A rough draft of the Constitution was put onto paper in August 1787.

Copies of the draft were given to convention deputies. Discussion over the Constitution began again. It lasted for five weeks. The convention organized a committee to make the final changes.

This portrait of George Washington was painted by artist Gilbert Stuart. George Washington was elected the first president of the United States after serving as president of the Constitutional Convention. It was at this convention that it was decided that a president should be elected. Washington was elected to serve the United States in its very first years.

On September 17, 1787, the members of the convention voted in favor of the Constitution. It was then sent to Congress. Congress agreed to pass the Constitution onto the states on September 28. Nine states had to approve of the document in order for it to be official.

On July 2, 1788, New Hampshire became the ninth state to ratify, or approve, the Constitution. The document was now official. The laws of the Constitution were ready to be put into action. The Continental Congress and state governments had to make way for the new government and laws. The Continental Congress ended its last official business in October. It decided that the new Congress would begin on March 4, 1789. It also decided that the president would be elected in February 1789. On December 15, 1791, the Bill of Rights was added to the Constitution. The Bill of Rights guarantees such things as freedom of speech and religion and the right to trial by jury.

The new government made by the Constitution was not perfect. Some issues, such as slavery, were overlooked or forgotten. Over time, Congress passed new amendments or changes to the Constitution.

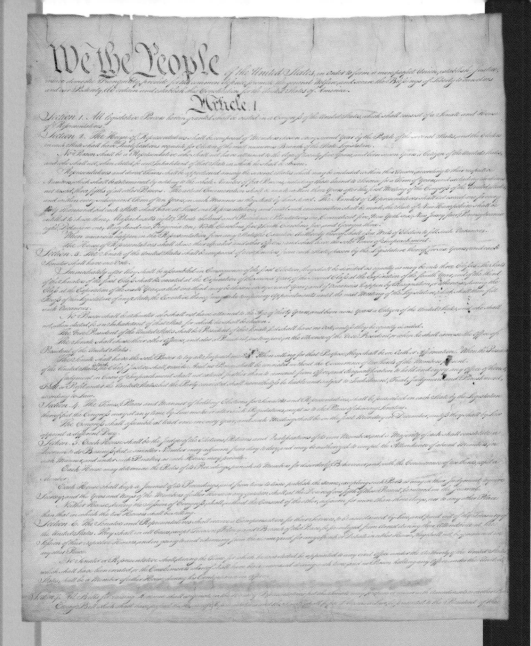

This is the Constitution of the United States in its original form. The original document is housed in Washington, DC, where many people go to see it each year. The Constitution outlines the laws by which the United States is governed. It is a very important part of United States history, and it is kept in special containers to ensure that it will be around for many years to come.

The amendments fixed any issues that were overlooked. For example, the Thirteenth Amendment made slavery illegal.

The Constitution is a very active part of our government today. Our court system still upholds, or keeps, the laws of the Constitution. Our Congress still follows the guidelines of the Constitution. The Constitution has remained strong over many years. Our nation still uses state constitutions as well. This is because some issues are local. These issues were not included in the United States Constitution. Local issues include school, public safety, and health matters. State constitutions list the rules of local issues. Massachusetts and New Hampshire still use their original state constitutions.

What does your state's constitution look like? What are the issues that are important to your state? How is it different or similar to the United States Constitution? How is it different or similar to other state constitutions? Finding out about your state constitution can be a fun adventure. You can begin your search at your local library.

Glossary

amend (uh-MEND) To add or change.

charter (CHAR-tuhr) A formal document that states the duties and rights of a group of people.

colonist (KAH-luh-nist) A person who lives in a newly settled area.

colony (KAH-luh-nee) A territory that has been settled by people from another country. The colony is controlled by that country.

committee (kuh-MIH-tee) A group of people with a common goal.

confederation (kuhn-feh-duh-RAY-shuhn) A group of people that have banded together because of similar beliefs.

Congress (KON-gres) The government body of the United States that makes laws.

Continental Congress (kon-tih-NEHN-tul KONG-gres) The first congress that included representatives from the colonies.

convention (kun-VEN-shuhn) When a group of people get together to form a plan or goal.

document (DOK-yoo-ment) A written paper that contains information or evidence.

draft (DRAFT) An initial version of a document.

guarantee (gahr-uhn-TEE) An assurance that a promise will be kept.

parliament (PAR-lih-mint) The group of people who have been elected to make laws in countries such as the United Kingdom.

ratify (RA-tih-fye) To agree to or approve of something officially.

representative (reh-prih-ZEN-tuh-tiv) Someone who is chosen to act or speak for others.

resource (REE-sors) Something that is valuable or useful.

symbol (SIM-bul) Something that stands for or represents something else.

unite (yoo-NYT) To come together and form a single unit.

vault (VAWLT) An enclosed, locked space used to guard important objects.

Web Sites

Due to the changing nature of Internet links, the Rosen Publishing Group, Inc., has developed an online list of Web sites related to the subject of this book. This site is updated regularly. Please use this link to access the list:

http://www.rosenlinks.com/lnan/uscesc

Primary Source Image List

Page 1: Lithograph of Independence Hall, by Theodore Poleni, October 30, 1875. Published by Tho Hunter, Lithographers.

Page 5: Painting by Howard Chandler Christie. Created in 1940. Housed in the U.S. Capitol Historical Society in Washington, DC.

Page 13: The document "The Declaration of Independence" was adopted by Congress on July 4, 1776. It is housed in the National Archives Building.

Page 15: Paper (note) by Thomas Jefferson, entitled "New York Constitution Revision, with Notes." It is housed in the Library of Congress.

Page 18: The document " The Articles of Confederation" was adopted by the Continental Congress on November 15, 1777. It is housed in the National Archives Building.

Page 20: Painting by John Trumball from 1792.

Page 22: Engraving by Alonzo Chappel from 1776. It is housed in the National Archives Building.

Page 24: Painting by Gilbert Stuart, published at the Albion, NY, Office in 1844.

Page 26: The document "The Constitution of the United States of America," signed on September 17, 1787, established the government of the United States. It is housed in the National Archives Building.

Index

About the Author

Holly Cefrey is a freelance writer. Her books have been awarded a place on the VOYA 2001 Nonfiction Honor List. She is a member of the Authors Guild and the Society of Children's Book Writers and Illustrators.

Thanks to Eliza and Rosen Publishing

Published in 2004 by The Rosen Publishing Group, Inc.
29 East 21st Street, New York, NY 10010

Copyright © 2004 by The Rosen Publishing Group, Inc.

First Edition

Library of Congress Cataloging-in-Publication Data

Cefrey, Holly.
The United States Constitution and early state constitutions: law and order in the new nation and states / by Holly Cefrey.— 1st ed.
        p. cm. — (Life in the new American nation)
Summary: Explains how the United States Constitution came to be, including events leading up to the Constitutional Convention, and explores how the Constitution changed the way the United States was governed.
Includes bibliographical references (p.) and index.
ISBN 0-8239-4042-X (lib. bdg.)
ISBN-0-8239-4260-0 (pbk. bdg.)
6-pack ISBN 0-8239-4273-2
1. United States—Constitution—Juvenile literature. 2. United States—Politics and government—1783–1789—Juvenile literature. 3. Constitutional history—United States—Juvenile literature. 4. Constitutions—United States—States—History—Juvenile literature. [1. United States. Constitution. 2. United States—Politics and government—1783–1789. 3. Constitutional law. 4. Constitutional history. 5. Constitutional law—United States—States.] I. Title. II. Series.
E303 .C35 2003
342.73'02—dc21

2002152843

Manufactured in the United States of America

Cover (left): The Constitution
Cover (right): Signing of the Declaration of Independence

Photo Credits: Cover (left and right), pp. 13, 15, 18, 20, 24, 26 courtesy of Library of Congress; pp. 1, 8 © Hulton/Archive/Getty Images; p. 5 © Architect of the Capitol; p. 10 © Bettmann/Corbis; p. 22 © National Archives and Records Administration.

Designer Nelson Sá; Editor: Eliza Berkowitz; Photo Researcher: Nelson Sá

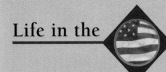

The United States Constitution and Early State Constitutions

Law and Order in the
New Nation and States

Holly Cefrey

rosen central

Primary Source™

The Rosen Publishing Group Inc., New York

New York
February 20th

"I'll always turn to the North!" said Lee.

He had been talking about the jungle trails on Barro Colorado Island, in Panama. Till my mind was a whirl of howling monkeys and motmots swinging, scarlet passion flowers and peccaries and blazing blue butterflies.

"Why don't we go to the tropics on our next vacation?"

"I'd rather show you the North," Lee insisted. "Alaska, the Aleutian Islands, Hudson Bay—"

"But the Arctic is either cold or swampy. I know I'd revel in constant balminess, and the bursts of tropic color—whole trees of golden blossoms, and faint rose—"

"Listen. I grant you the tropics are beautiful. But the design is too intricate. Now, in the North you may have one line for the tundra, one for a maroon hill, and another for the snow mountains. Only three lines in the whole landscape. But *what* lines they are! I tell you, the Arctic has character, and composition."

"Yes, my lamb, I know you like the Arctic. But *I* can't revel in starkness. I do want to see solitary places, Lee. But I want to be able to lie down on my back and look at the sky—"

9

"You can't lie down, or even sit down, out of doors in Panama. If you stop one minute, the ticks and red bugs get you."

"Oh—" I was rather baffled. "Anyway, I like trees."

Lee shook his head. "I'll have to take you to the southern limit of the North! What about my state? What about northern Minnesota sometime?"

"That's not arctic."

"It's not so far from it. The muskeg comes down there, and we certainly have winter weather. . . . I wish we could see it this minute; snow means something *there*." Lee looked with intense scorn at the perfectly adequate snow storm outside our windows, whirling around corners and blurring the towers far up the street quite recklessly enough, it seemed to me.

"I wish we were there now," he repeated. "I'd like you to see the pines and tamaracks in three feet of snow. You ought to hear the snow screech under the sled runners, and trees crack in the silence, at twenty below zero."

"I'll go in summer," I said firmly.

"Or early spring, with the horned larks on the fence posts along the snowy roads. Or October. We could hunt prairie chickens then, through the fields."

I began to think of all the things Lee had told me of his Minnesota home. The great stretches of woods where he had hunted deer in his boyhood. The immense skies. Seven Oaks, the house of hand-hewn logs, built by some pioneer and discovered by Lee's mother and father when they came to that country; a house set, with its oaks around it, in a deep curve of the Mississippi. The Mississippi itself, only a small river in that northern land, where Lee used to watch logs floating down to the mills, and the stern-wheeled steamers traveling in summer. The old state road, where the four-horse teams hauled provisions to the lumber camps all through the winter. . . .

10

"I do want to see Minnesota before it loses every trace of pioneer life. But I'll go in summer," I reiterated.

"Of course, if we went in summer I could take you into the Arrowhead country," Lee admitted.

"Yes! What about that canoe country? After all your tales and promises, Othello! Have you ever taken me?"

"Well, why not go? This summer?"

We looked at each other questioningly. Then hopefully.

Perhaps we really shall.

Sunday, February 27th

It has been raining furiously all day long. I'm glad it has.

This afternoon we unearthed the canoe country maps. Lee has shown them to me before and I've always looked at them with sedate interest — never with the catches of breath they gave me today.

There's one huge map of the lake country in general, all the way from the international boundary to the Arctic and from Lake Superior to the Lake of the Woods, nearly to Winnipeg. Another is a detailed map of the Arrowhead itself, the Quetico reserve in Canada and the Superior National Forest in Minnesota, the borderland of both countries. Then smaller maps, some of which Lee helped to make.

I can hardly believe in that country. Hundreds and hundreds of lakes scattered through forest, like pieces of a mammoth jigsaw puzzle scattered over a table. Scraps of rivers lace the lakes together. There are no roads, no paths except short portages; one can travel only by water.

We hung over the maps till I could see curled waves and minute pine trees all over them. I found "This Man's Lake" and "That Man's Lake," with a forlorn little "No Man's Lake" tucked in between and an "Other Man's Lake" farther on. We traced out all Lee's former canoe trips, and he showered me with incredible numbers of old snapshots, to illustrate his explanations. They were most beautiful photographs.

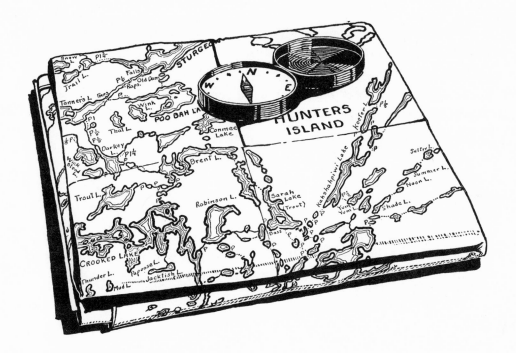

"Lee, we *must* go," I cried.

He disappeared, and came back, to my amazement, with a stepladder. It seemed a peculiar answer to my exclamation. Were we to take off immediately, with the stepladder for airplane? But no. Mounting it, he began to excavate the top recesses of the studio closet.

"What *are* you after?"

". . . see what I've saved from my equipment," he muttered, and began to hand down the canvas bundles and packsacks which have always been mysteries to me.

I don't know how we progressed from studio to living room, but soon we had the latter ornamented with a small tent, an axe, a bevy of pails that fitted into each other with marvelous precision, tin plates, scores of small cloth bags ("you carry all the food in those; you can't pack the extra weight of boxes and cans"), fishing tackle, a coffee pot, a skillet, besides the maps and pictures scattered like leaves after a storm.

Of course it had to be the immaculate Bartons who called at this moment, with two German ornithologists in tow. It couldn't have been any of our intimate acquaintances.

To brush aside Mrs. Barton's magnificent pretense that there was nothing at all extraordinary about our living room *décor*, we had to explain, "We're going on a canoe trip this summer."

So we are committed now. What fun!

Duluth, Minnesota
August 21st

I've never been so cold in my life. I wear my fur coat all the time. If this is what Duluth is like in August what must it be in January!

"Of course," people tell me cheerily, "you'll be much colder camping out."

And I can't take this fur coat with me.

"Three weeks!" they say. "And you've never camped before? Better make it one!"

Three weeks does take careful planning. We must remember everything; there is no place to buy or borrow. And to pack house and furnishings and food inside one small canoe is quite puzzling. Today we've been sorting out our equipment in Aunt Mary's garden, while the next-door children ran around and over us like beetles in wild excitement.

Lee's canoe is intact and is ready to ship to Winton. Our tent is so small it's laughable. Seven by seven, with a ground cloth to match, it ties up in front by one rope to a pole or tree. We're taking an air mattress, an air pillow, and a blanket roll.

There are three packsacks, one for food, another for clothes (with a waterproof bag that holds our toilet articles and a small medicine case), and a third for miscellaneous articles — fishing tackle, films, Lee's sketching outfit, my notebooks, canoe glue, an axe, flashlights, etc. We aren't allowed to take a gun.

14

We have gone over our list of provisions again and again. The food must be nourishing and yet as concentrated in bulk as it can possibly be. Each purchase is now neatly tied into its little cloth bag. Except the butter — it goes in a can. This is our list:

5 lbs ham	2 lbs salt (we salt the fish to
5 lbs bacon	keep it)
2 lbs dried beef	1 can pepper
1 can corned beef	4 lbs sweet chocolate
1 can veal loaf	2 lbs cheese
3 cans Crisco	2 cans soluble coffee
2 lbs butter	1 can lemon powder (for
10 lbs flour	lemonade)
1 can baking powder	5 lbs brown sugar (for syrup
4 loaves bread	as well as sugar)
1 package rye crisp	1 can powdered milk
2 lbs raisins	2 bars soap
3 lbs apricots	1 cake Sapolio
3 lbs prunes	6 candles
4 lbs dried beans	1 box matches (another in
2 lbs dried peas (a mistake)	miscellaneous pack)

It seems what the women's magazines might call a Meager Menu. Of course if we were taking a guide we could live much more luxuriously, with canned vegetables and even an oven. But a guide would bring civilization into our trip; we would have a buffer between us and the wilderness. As it is, we're facing nature as I, at least, never have before in my life.

As for reading, I'm afraid I'm going to do less of that in the next few weeks than I've ever done in the same length of time. I have three paperbound reprints, and an old copy of *The King's Henchman,* which hasn't any cover!

I did want to take along some of the vivid stories of explorers and fur

traders, especially the earliest ones, Radisson and Du Luth, for instance, and La Vérendrye (Pierre Gaultier de Varennes de la Vérendrye, to be exact), who with his sons built a string of forts along this route.

Most of all I wanted to take the account Radisson wrote for some of his patrons in England. Radisson was a dashing scamp, perhaps the first white man ever to set foot in this Arrowhead country, and his charm and high spirits (to say nothing of his imagination!) are evident in these *Voyages* of his. Nor can I bear to leave behind the quaint journals of traders like Peter Pond, Macdonell, Hugh Faries, and Nicholas Garry, exact and enthralling accounts of early canoe trips. But books are far too bulky. I must be content with the notebook into which I've copied my favorite passages.

I've warned my family at home that they won't hear from us for three weeks. We'll probably be able to send them some word, Lee says, but since we may not have a chance, it is better for them not to expect letters.

Thursday, August 25th

We have started!

I did appreciate our train's thoughtfulness in leaving Duluth so early yesterday morning; I could not have waited another half-day.

In the early afternoon we disembarked at Winton. Quite unreasonably, I'd been taking it for granted that we would start out from a long pier by a summer inn, with gay launches about and bright flags flying, people promenading in smart sport clothes, so that I'd feel rather conspicuous and shabby in my corduroys and packsacks, before we escaped from sight.

So I felt relieved, though astonished, when we left the train, to find only a dingy country town. The single unusual sight was an Indian family boarding the train: a fat chief, three women in scarlet and orange, and a small Indian boy with a huge basket of blueberries. One of the women

17

had a papoose strapped to her back, which rather surprised me. I thought that custom had vanished long ago.

Lee saw that our canoe came out of the baggage car safely, and we went up to the general store to collect our last supplies. I changed from my traveling things to my corduroy outfit in the attic storeroom, we left our civilized baggage there, and the storekeeper loaded us, our canoe, and packsacks into a truck, took us out, and dropped us along a country road. It all seemed very casual.

Beyond a russet barn, a lake of gentian blue shimmered bright down a grassy hill. We carried everything down to a sketchy dock, we put our canoe in the water, our packs and ourselves in the canoe, and started off.

It was as simple as that.

At first, as we swung out and dipped our paddles into liquid sapphire, the ghosts of the sawmills which used to be so busy here stood all about us. When we got beyond their ruin, and passed summer cottages and boathouses for an hour or more, it was like being on the water at home. This was a mild beginning for adventure.

But when we came to our first portage path, and I helped to unload the canoe, and took the shadowy way with a pack on my shoulders, I felt this was a new experience after all. I carried the clothes pack, Lee took the miscellaneous sack on his back and lifted the canoe — with the paddles lashed in — over his head, so that the yoke fitted to his shoulders. The second trip he took the food pack and blanket roll, while I carried the camera, field glasses, and other odds and ends. I liked tramping over the portage twice with loads; I liked the smell of hot pines and the curve of ferns, the glimpse of dazzling water ahead.

We went down the second lake. Lee settled the packs lower, to lessen wind resistance as well as to steady the canoe. By sunset we had landed on a scrap of peninsula, I had watched Lee cut down a leafy poplar for our first tent pole, and had cooked my first supper over a campfire. Afterward, as we sat on the rocks in the afterglow, a muskrat swam across the

duskiness — our first wild animal. I waved a benediction at him before I went to bed.

Before I left New York, I had wondered whether it would not seem a little desolate to sleep on the ground in a tent, and if the night noises would keep me awake and restless. Even Nicholas Garry's diary did not entirely reassure me. "Nor Ghosts, nor Rattlesnakes, nor Spiders," he said, comfortingly, "nothing can prevent the fatigued Voyageur from sleeping." I had only hoped that I would be as unperturbed.

But now, as I crept between the blankets, I was far too drowsy to realize I was sleeping out of doors for the first time in my life. I went to sleep without a thought for my surroundings.

But this morning, the white mist about us, the exultant laughter of the loons (Lee's favorite birds in this country), made me feel I was really in a different land.

I've just learned how to break camp. There are two inviolable rules.

First, to leave the camping place as
unscarred as possible. Every bit of litter must
be burned or carefully hidden, so that we haven't made the forest uglier
by our presence.

Second, and even more important, every spark of fire must be completely extinguished. To cause immense destruction or perhaps death, because we hadn't taken the trouble to carry another pail of water, or wait
an extra minute, would be horrible.

We are starting now on our first long day's voyage. It is a blue and
immaculate morning, with a quiet wind pacing along with us.

I insist that I should be initiated, as each new *voyageur* was on enter-
ing this country, by being sprinkled with a cedar bough, with appropriate

ceremony, even if we can't manage "a dozen of gunshots fired one after another in an Indian manner." But Lee says that since I haven't a trapping license I am not really a *voyageur*, only a *coureur de bois*. Or should it be *coureuse?*

The loons are flying above us, still laughing. I would like to laugh as jubilantly, at all the people who said I wouldn't like a canoe trip!

Late afternoon

Now we are in the true forest; no more cabins since we left the forest ranger's, where we got our Canadian fishing license, this noon. We have been following the international boundary marks, which trace the ancient canoe route of the Indians. This morning we landed on a sand beach in the United States, to go swimming in the green and orange water; so we decided we would make camp in Canada this afternoon.

What a way to travel—no trains to catch, no traffic to annoy us, no towns to reach by evening, no appointments to remember! We wander anywhere our whims take us, through these lakes and rivers.

Freedom surrounds us. We are finding more than peace here. This is an authentic and profound release from modern intricacies.

I caught the rhythm of paddling today, so that the paddle, the canoe, and I were all one. The monotony of the dip, the push, and the swing has a peculiar fascination after a while. But my shoulders and back are still remembering it.

Our camp tonight is under an enormous white pine, by rapids of dark green glass and snow. Norway pines darken the rocky hill. The ground is covered with blueberry plants, thick with blue lusters. It seems a crime to eat these berries of lapis lazuli, but when we discovered them we never thought of aesthetic scruples—we seized them with both hands.

I speak with such authority about the white and Norway pines, because I've just been learning, from shining examples on the shore, the differences between them. The white is the one with the beautiful horizontal

masses. Its three-sided needles, blue-green and
pliable, come in clusters of five, and its grayish bark
is rough and deeply grooved in old trees. The Norway is straight and tall
(though it cannot reach the height of the largest white pines) with a
reddish trunk. Its stiff dark green needles, flat on one side and rounded
on the other, come in clusters of two.

I've just been down the rocks picking up decorative pine cones for my
campfire. There was a runaway little kingfisher on a twig, pretending to
be an austere and steady fisherman. But he had his father's best white col-
lar on, much too big for him—it came to his eyes—while his hair stuck
up straight with excitement and his tiny feet clutched the twig so ar-
dently I know he was inwardly overwhelmed by his venture.

Lee is fishing too. He has gone over to a narrow island to fish the rapids. Two packsacks lie inside the tent; the third one, with the food and cooking things, keeps me company here. We'll have pancakes and coffee tonight, fish perhaps, certainly blueberries.

Night

While Lee was across the rapids, he caught a ponderous pickerel, and also caught the fishhook in his hand. It came out docilely enough, thank heaven, but when he reached our shore he was bleeding all over the canoe and the rocks and moss, though he was too proud of his capture to notice it. At home I would probably have shrieked and swooned, but here, as there was no one to dash to my aid, I bandaged him up in such a coolly efficient manner that I stood in awed admiration of myself.

As I was serving supper on the rock, I remembered Garry's description of his table, and scrambled in the pack to get my notebook, so that I could read aloud to Lee:

"Our Dinner Table was a hard Rock, no Table Cloth could be cleaner and the surrounding Plants and beautiful Flowers sweetening the Board. Before us the Waterfall, wild romantic, bold. The River Winnipic here impeded by Mountainous Rocks appears to have found a Passage through the Rocks and these, as if still disputing the Power of Water, show their Heads, adding to the rude Wildness of the Scene, producing Whirlpools, Foam loud Noise, and chrystal Whiteness beautifully contrasted with the Black Pine."

It's just the same. What a chance this is, to see granite shores which haven't changed at all, in the three hundred years that have transformed Manhattan from a quiet coast to the most amazing city on earth! To step back in time, and see this country, as the first explorers saw it, as the Indians did when they were its conquerors! Here, one hundred years *is* but a day.

Lee liked the "Whirlpools, Foam loud Noise, and chrystal Whiteness" as much as I did, so I went on to read him Radisson's description of the moose — he calls it sometimes an Eland and sometimes an Oriniack.

23

"Most of the woods and forests are very thick, so that it was in some places as darke as in a cellar, by reason of the boughs of trees. The snow that falls, being very light, hath not the strength to stopp the eland, which is a mighty strong beast, much like a mule, having a tayle cutt off 2 or 3 or 4 thumbes long, the foot cloven like a stagge. He has a muzzle mighty bigge."

Here Radisson branches off to the "Buff" which "is a furious animal. One must have a care of him . . ." But surely he is talking of the moose again when he says,

"I have seene of their hornes that a man could not lift them from of the ground. They are branchy and flatt in the midle, of which the wildman makes dishes that can well hold 3 quarts. These hornes fall off every yeare, and it's a thing impossible that they will grow againe."

How can I wait to see an Oriniack!

Friday

We had a sunny and strenuous day's canoeing, with many portages. One very long one, in the late morning, to avoid a series of rapids. The path was so constantly sunny, through small bushes, asters, and goldenrod, up and down hot little hills with rocks to stumble over, that two trips seemed unbearable. I tried to call up visions of La Vérendrye and his sons stalking along this path, of Radisson, debonair and blithe. But I could only picture them in snow or rain or gloom of night. I don't believe they could cope with heat either.

Lunch was on a small hot island under some very unsatisfactory jack pines. These are scrub pines and take all sorts of shapes; we've even seen several solitary ones trying to look like apple trees. How we would have appreciated one like that! But these were contrary creatures, too thin for shade. I felt like shaking shadows out of them.

By keeping our luncheon provisions (just picnic things, cheese crackers, chocolate, and raisins) in the top of the food pack, we don't need to unpack every noon. Simpler and simpler. So after lunching lightly

and making lemonade with our lemon powder, we allowed ourselves a short nap. Then on through the hot afternoon.

The rivers were like Peter Pond's favorites, "Verey Gental but Verey Sarpentine." And the lakes were motionless. But we weren't; we were hot and dripping. Who was it told me I'd freeze in this canoe country?

Then Lee decided to teach me to paddle and steer at the same time, and I was not a success. My exertions and Lee's hootings were becoming quite unbearable when, just after three, we turned north away from the international route, and found paradise.

In the first place, we came to a cliff and felt real shade for the first time since early morning. Here we drifted awhile, dipping our hands in the water, and cooling our vivid faces. Then we went on into three small circle lakes which lay, one after another, like strung sapphires.

The island we have chosen to camp on is in the second lake. The first is only half enchanted, but this is wholly so; and as for the third one, it is so bewitched you can't even talk there. I know; we've tried it.

Our own lake is decorated with big round green lily pads and small oval ones of rose and gold. The pine trees stand sedately around it, trailing their reflections in the rippled water, and a flock of little flapper ducks, too young to fly, had it for their own until we came.

Down a very zigzag path—for I was still steering—we came to our chosen island, and its long shadows looked very welcome after the sun's bright glare and Lee's admonitory one. Our tent is on the northern tip of the island. We look out past a great sweep of pine bough to the waters of our lake and the silent misty one beyond.

This is the moment, I think, when I've really given my heart to our canoe country, though I've been entranced with it from the first. But here its special quality of wild innocence touches me sharply and deeply.

I should very much like to live here forever. It's sorcery. It's not our world at all; it's another star.

This evening we set out to acquaint ourselves with our territories. Back to the first lake of the chain, where there were beaver houses to investigate. Then across our own lake again, laughing and talking nonsense.

But at the inlet to the third, we fell silent. If we didn't make a noise, Lee muttered, pretending he could talk if he wanted to, we might see a deer.

The water was without a ripple. Its candid ring was edged with tall bulrushes, spare dark whips exactly reflected. Great pines stood up around it in lovely broken lines, and down a narrow marsh we saw a great blue heron motionless in the tufted grass.

We slipped without a sound through the tranquillity. The rushes slanted above our heads as we floated by.

We came to the channel of an ethereal river, vanishing among the reeds. There was no breath of sound. Great white boulders gleamed here and there in the clear waterway. The rushes massed around us. Along silent curves we slid, on and on, until at last a small rapids rushed down from the black sanctuary of the forest.

Its foamy course broke the silence; we took a breath, and turned our canoe homeward.

It was dusk now, but a faint clear light still held. As we drifted back through the high reeds, great horizontal ripples came slowly toward us through the crystal water. It gave me the oddest sensation — our canoe seemed to be rising straight up into the twilight air. But that would not have been unnatural, after all, in this strange place.

We heard a great horned owl call, far away. Darkness was coming down the hills. In the pale water before me, an otter curved momentarily, and the silver wake of a beaver flashed, far down the other lake.

28

At the inlet, we could see our small white tent glimmering in the center of the island, in the center of the lake, in the center of the forest. Here was the center of the world.

Saturday

It's cool this morning. I'm writing this in a tall pine wood. Giant pines range up a long hill, with clean open spaces between the bronze trunks instead of all the undergrowth and ferns and twisted branches we usually have. Morning sunlight falls down to the matted needles in bars of brown sunniness and gold mist. The wind tastes fresh, pungent, and wild.

How utterly different this forest land is from the other two I've loved! Fontainebleau, a medieval dream forest (of course we saw it in April); the New Forest, the essence of England's beauty, where Robin Hood might appear down any glade. This country never knew a medieval time; it came straight from the primeval into today. And as for Robin Hood, I can't quite picture him scrambling over logs or hunting moose in a canoe.

We've been up the river. We portaged past the rapids — it seems so easy to portage when the baggage is home in camp! — and on up the stream. We found grassy banks, with spruce behind them, and then burned-over hills, bare and haunted. Giant trunks lay along the banks, their roots and branches distorted in the air. The river became so persistent in its stones and boulders that we could barely push through.

We met our first pileated woodpecker here, high on a charred pine. (At least, *he* was on the charred pine.) He is very shy and is found in the wildest places, so I was glad to have a chance to gaze at him.

He was a stunning bird, about twice as large as our red-headed woodpecker; black with a pattern of white on wings and neck, and a flashing red crest. He looked so powerful I longed to see him attack a tree, for he cuts and chisels like mad, hanging on by his feet and using his whole body for a hammer. Chips and strips of bark fly in every direction, and he sometimes rips off pieces a foot long.

30

But he didn't perform for me. He went away instead, flashing the great spots of white beneath his wings as he flew, and left me lost in admiration.

Lee says the courtship dance of the pileated woodpecker is most extraordinary. The male and female meet on a treetop, spread their pinions wide (they're between two and three feet across) and hop and balance and bow to each other. Sometimes they kiss or feed each other, and then begin their posturing again. What a strange spectacle it would be, against the sky! Often they fly up and wheel in circles through the air, with fluttering wings and pointed crests, and then come down to dance again on the branches. I wish I could see them. I wonder if they look as joyful as the black and white lapwings we saw tumbling down the sky in England.

Saturday Evening

This afternoon we went down to the Painted Rocks and climbed the cliff, to a lake that was lying obstinately on top of the hill, instead of at the bottom where it belonged! We found a very jungle-y place where something had been wallowing. And on the cliff edge were the most enormous blueberries in the world. Hothouse blueberries, almost as big as grapes.

Then, in the canoe, we floated under the Painted Rocks.

On the overhanging cliffs, Lee pointed out to me the vague outlines of moose, in red pigment. The first explorers saw these too. In Macdonell's journal he tells of some at Derraud's Rapids between Lake Huron and the Ottawa River:

"The figure of a man standing over an animal that lays under him, with a sun on one side and a moon on the other . . . A little farthur on is at least 16 figures of different animals standing promiscuously together on the face of a steep Rock . . . painted with some kind of Red Paint."

Above the drawings was a crack into which the Indians used to shoot their arrows. A friend of Lee's once climbed up and found arrowheads there.

It's threatening rain tonight, and Lee is making the tent snug, seeing that the wall canvas is tucked under the floor cloth on every side, and digging a shallow trench around us.

Sunday, August 28th

It did rain last night. It is raining today.

I woke in the night to the sound of rain pounding its tiny fists against the canvas so near our heads. I couldn't believe I was out in such a fragile shelter in the middle of a storm. Such frail walls to hold off such a bombardment. But our tent seemed to be intact and dry, so serenely I folded my hands and went to sleep again.

When I awoke this morning the lake was silver gray, and gray mist dimmed the forests. Our merganser ducks, feeling important, were steamboating like mad around the lake. Twenty-four of them in a proud little line, making reckless splatters in the rain.

We made a pygmy fire of pine cones and twigs, sheltering it between two stones in the tent opening. Just enough of a campfire for hot coffee. With it we ate ham and rye crisp and apricots, and watched from our refuge for ducks or deer. Only some Indians came past in a heavily laden canoe, bound, I suppose, for a reservation up on Lac la Croix.

I had to struggle against an idiotic pity for our canoe, lying on the shore, upside down and shining wet, in the plunging rain! I have become

32

very fond of this companion of ours,
which carries us along so resolutely.
All the more because one is so
thwarted in an affection for a canoe
—there's nothing to do for it. If I
could only give it a loose rein, or feed it hay or gasoline! But it is completely independent. I can only pat it slightly now and then.

Later it rained more gently, so we put on our raincoats and went out
to fish. I decided that fishing in the rain is far more glamorous than fishing in the sun, for the lake was gray moire, the mistiness changed from
gray to soft Madonna blue, and the distant islands had dimmed to phan-
toms of faint violet. The rain made a tiny patting sound on the lily leaves
and on our hats.

An osprey circled over the lake searching for fish. Then he sat in the
top of a pine and looked down meditatively into the water. *Le Penseur.*
I don't know what he caught, but I caught four pike, a bass, and a water
lily as lovely as an ivory carving.

33

It is now sitting in a tin cup under the dripping pine, looking as out of place as a duchess in a wheelbarrow.

Monday, August 29th

We arose at the hour of five this morning, to chase a moose we had heard in the night.

Never hear a cow moose in the night, when you don't know what it is! It is the most blood-freezing sound, a wild and wailing whoop, uncanny as Dracula. I heard it first at midnight. "Lee! What is that?"

"Well," he said thoughtfully, "it doesn't sound exactly like wolves!"

If *he* doesn't know what it is, I thought, after all his canoe trips!

"Lee," I said, after thinking wistfully of guns and revolvers, "Lee, where is the axe?"

"Down on the shore by the canoe."

And then that awful howl, much nearer this time. But there wasn't anything to be done and I went back to sleep. However, Lee, hearing it again before daylight, decided it was a lovelorn moose. So he woke me up and we started out to find it.

We couldn't see a thing beyond the rocks where the canoe lay. It was fantastic, launching the canoe into an immensity of fog; we were paddling in a white cloud. But to my relief we didn't fall through.

After a time we got the vaguest of shore lines; by then the lake was so thick with rushes that we slid along through them as if we were paddling in a grassy meadow. We found the mouth of the phantom river and went along, surprising a flock of black ducks and two great blue heron. There were no moose.

On our way back, a deer stirred in the grass along the shore. Lee paddled very gently toward her, while I found I couldn't manage my breath, to say nothing of the field glasses. As we drew near, Lee took only a stroke now and then when she lowered her head to eat, till at last we were in the reeds beside her. When we glided up close to the delicate

creature she gazed astonished. Then she whirled off among the upspringing birches.

I had wondered, I'll admit, if a three weeks' trip might not seem monotonous part of the time, in such a complete solitude. But I was wrong. Our life is as full here, for the time being, as it is in New York, with all its companions from every part of the world, its great art and music, its floodtides of ideas.

For every second, every inch, of this experience is filled with utter harmony. We take our way wherever we like; the animals and birds are as good company as one could ask; and if we tried we couldn't find an unsightly spot or a jarring note.

No despairs are here. And no man-made dangers. The bright eyes of the beasts need only look for their natural enemies, and we ourselves can forget all the world's turmoils and antagonisms. This absolute freedom gives every hour an intense lucidity.

Tuesday

We broke camp yesterday morning, breaking our hearts as well, as we left our circle lakes behind us. I couldn't have left if it had been as ethereal as usual, but it was a dull and forbidding morning, with clouds of iron ranging low. After we were well away, however, the day forgot its sullenness.

All day long we came west through the intricacies of Crooked Lake. Lovely river ways, wide stretches of cornflower water, studded islands; shores ranging from great bare hills just touched with delicate green by the young birches and poplars to massive tangled forest.

This was a day with people in it. First, in the morning, we met two boys from St. Paul, going out. They offered to take our mail, so the two canoes clung together for a while, in mid-lake, while Lee talked to the boys about their experiences and I scribbled an enthusiastic letter to the family.

Then at noon, as we passed a low island with a camp on it, we saw a lone man dancing and leaping and shouting wildly. He wasn't in pain, nor were his shouts ecstasy; they were just yells.

In the twilight this would have been quite eerie; even at noon it was grotesque enough — that tousled figure, leaping in the sun.

We didn't know whether he was drunk, or touched by the silence of this country. We had a Chicago friend, a man who had always lived in cities, who came here for an outing but went out the second day. He said he couldn't stand the feeling that there wasn't anyone beyond a hill. Sometimes, they say, when a ranger is here alone for months, he goes slightly mad from the solitary unconfinement.

So, as the dancer didn't call to us for help, I was glad to hurry past this island.

We ate our lunch farther along, with me keeping a wary eye out for a delirious canoe. Much to Lee's amusement, the wretch.

The afternoon freshened, with a gusty wind and high-piled clouds. At first we had many islands, but later in the afternoon we came to the western end of the lake, which was almost a "traverse," as the *voyageurs* called a wide stretch of water. The waves grew choppy enough to make it quite exciting. We lurched and shipped water until I had to bail, for the first time in our journey. I was glad Lee had had so much experience in canoeing.

Lee remembered a very beautiful point near the Curtain Falls, but as we approached it we could see two white tents in among its pines. Baffled — why were *people* around here, anyway? — we went past almost to the falls and found a camp site on a small stony bay, with drooping jack pines on it and a heavy forest behind.

Here we are two Gullivers in Lilliput. We have a great stir of wild life around us, in an extremely small way. Chipmunks by the score gallop around, mad with curiosity. Chickadees swarm in the pines, right side up or upside down, it doesn't seem to matter; their *dee-dee-dee*'s are con-

39

stant. Starring the camp are dragonflies of every kind, bronze ones, gigantic emerald ones almost as big as the chickadees, small ones of gossamer blue, which are my special favorites.

And when I went down the shore to get driftwood, I ran into a migration of yellow warblers, hundreds of them, flicking in and out of the foliage like yellow sparks.

I sat down on a ledge to watch them. My hand against the harsh surface made me think of the stones themselves.

The rock formation of this whole country, I read somewhere, is part of the great Canadian Shield, so called because its surface of more than a million square miles, surrounding Hudson Bay on three sides and coming down into the United States at this point, is in the shape of a vast shield. This shield is of pre-Cambrian rocks, the oldest on the crust of the earth. From 48,000,000 to 1,710,000,000 years old! Those figures made a deep impression.

I looked back to those primordial ages, with the sundered stone around me — the stone that is the most ancient thing that we can see or touch in our world. The vastness of this shield and its antiquity was overwhelming me, when the *chee*-ing of the warblers made me turn back to them. Their evanescent yellow feathers flitted as gaily as ever through the cobweb green. I picked up my firewood and went home.

We had our supper on the rocks by the water, with impulsive chipmunks crowding us. One especially, dashing in and out of woodpecker holes like a miniature clown, distracted me terribly from my cooking. After supper I began to wash my dishes, but there was an afterglow of such luminous peach-gold that we left the dishes unregarded on the shore. Floating off into the spacious evening, without a ripple in the clear light above or below us, we set out to see Curtain Falls.

The falls, rough and dangerous, hypnotized me. The black smoothness of the water, just before it curved over the falls, was savagely elemental. We stayed till dark watching it, the spray and the green underswing; listening to the loons call.

When we got back to our point, we still had the Lilliputians about. Two tiny wood mice came out to clear away our crumbs. They were comic things, with their big eyes and round fuzzy ears and bits of whiskers. I felt quite guilty, liking them so much, when I shriek at house mice.

But I was in a liking mood. I even enjoyed washing my dishes, with the black night all about and stars in my rinsing water.

We saw the red sun come up this morning, through white mist. Our customary breakfast, blueberries, flapjacks, bacon, and coffee, tasted unusually good out on our rocks, even though the chipmunks chanted crossly at us because there were no prune seeds. After breakfast we went to Roland Lake portage to find a moose swamp Lee remembered. We found the swamp but no moose.

Only more loons. But they repaid us. I had never before been near enough to see how they run along the water's surface before they fly, and their spattering strides across the lake amused me enormously. Nor had I known before that they can vary their specific gravity at will, so that they float either with their spotted black and white bodies showing or with just the sleek black heads and striped necks above water.

We made a game of timing their long dives under water — they are magnificent submarines — and seeing who could guess how long they would stay submerged. One stayed under four minutes and a half — he was our champion. But they have been known to stay as long as eight minutes.

I hadn't realized before that loons are strictly water birds. They can barely hobble on land, though they make such swift runs on the lakes. And their flying seems to be done under water as well as in the air, for they use their wings as well as their feet in their long dives. They are all mixed up about locomotion. I turn giddy thinking of them, soaring in reverse, with fish about them.

Lee says they have many calls. The common laughing call, *hoo-hoo-hoo-hoo*, and the night call we have heard. Then there is a storm call, and what is known as the "silly song," as well as shorter notes.

Coming back, we met the people who are camping on the point. There were two canoes, a couple in one, in the other a guide and a fat man who, believe it if you can, wore a big white life preserver! He was

42

quite complacent about it, but the red-headed guide looked as shamefaced as a small boy does when a doll is forced upon him.

Wednesday, August 31st

These voyaging days are translucent with joy. When we start out in the morning, the earth has such a before-Eden look that it seems a shame to shake the dew from the blueberries or strike our paddles into the sleeping water. Thrusting on into sun-filled channels; drifting into green-needled embrasures where chickadees are buoyant; landing on a beach to bathe and to read the overnight paw prints — it is all intoxicating.

Now we have left the smooth pine slopes and the great bare hills of stone. We have come to rugged shores, ancient pines, and huge creviced rocks, rich in tone, padded deep with hoary moss and gray-green lichens. When the lakes are calm, they reflect the most glowing colors, dark wines and purples and crimsons, deep blues and greens, that we haven't noticed on the banks.

Only after we have seen the pure colors in the water do we look up and distinguish them in the tree trunks and cliffs, where we have seen only browns and greens because we weren't expecting anything else. An artist once told me that if you really want to see the color of a landscape you should stand on your head. This of course is practically the same thing.

We are camping on a jagged island in Lac la Croix.

Until now I have been very amenable about our camps. I've liked to go along and never know when Lee would say, "Why not camp here?"

But that is changed. Yesterday on the Curtain Falls portage — by the way, have I said how deeply I approve of portages? After miles of sunny waters, to have a chance to use your legs instead of your arms for propulsion, to plunge into a crisp, shadowed path, sundering ferns and bushes, brushing spiced boughs, a turquoise lake behind, unknown water ahead, feet clinking on the stones! In our doubled trips across, I never get quite

44

used to leaving half of all our worldly
goods sitting unprotected on the rocks. Nor can
I ever take for granted the wood fragrance, so different
from the smell of the air on the lakes. I have pine scent inextricably mixed
with portages now; one will always make me remember the other.

As I was saying, on this portage we met a couple who had been fishing
for deep lake trout. The four of us sat down by the black curves and foam
white of the rapids and talked, mostly about trout. However, Mrs. Morse
did mention casually that they had seen no moose this year but that
wolves seemed unusually prevalent, and so they had preferred to camp on
islands.

So now I prefer to camp on islands too.

I can't help it. Lee teases me, and I know it's foolish, that the wolves
can swim if they're really hungry, that they only get ravenous in winter,

and that even in winter it is extremely doubtful that they ever attack man. But still Mrs. Morse's words reverberate in the air. And after all, why *not* camp on islands?

They're much more interesting than mainlands, which run on and on in an aimless sort of way. Each island we meet has an individuality of its own, serene or careless or aloof. We saw an innocently wanton one clad in nothing but two daisy plants.

Our present island was bequeathed to us by the Morses.

It's just beyond Bottle Portage. It may be the one where Macdonell "Killed a cub Bear and slept in sight of the Mai." The mai was a lobstick or maypole, a favorite landmark of the *voyageur*, made by cutting away most of the branches of a tall tree. I like to think what welcome signs they must have been, just as the international boundary markers are hailed by us with joy.

This is an island with an escarpment, rather high and harsh, around three sides. To the west we have a small harbor, a semicircle of flat clean-washed stones. The center has an open space for our tent, the rest is inexorably wooded, and the thick dark moss under the trees is wonderful to walk on barefoot.

How much more sensitive we are to feeling in this primitive environment! In fact, all five senses are much more wide awake. Of course, one would expect seeing and hearing to be more enjoyable here, since there are only pleasant sights and sounds. And taste is proverbially keener out of doors.

But how much more I notice the touch of things! The smooth paddle in my hand, the shock of cold water on my face, the texture of rough sticks and pine cones when I pick up firewood. The slimness of pine needles in my fingers, the springy turf or hard granite when I step.

And the increased keenness in the sense of smell. I wish we had a better word for *smell*—one that didn't suggest a disagreeable sensation! *Scent, fragrance, odor*, they are all too sweet, too flowery. No, *smell* is what I mean, the different way that early morning smells, and twilight. The changes one forest path can give you as you walk along, the scent of wet green leaves, and dried brown ones, of mushrooms, and crushed grass. . . .

Last night it was cold. There was a hint of a new moon in the apple-green sky, and a wind in the pines all night long. Snug in my blankets, I could imagine that the branches above us still held faint echoes of war drums, or the songs of the *voyageurs:*

> *"Quand j'étais chez mon Père,*
> *Petite Janeton,*
> *Il m'envoyait à la fontaine*
> *Pour pêcher du poisson.*
> *La Violette Dandon, oh!*
> *La Violette dandé. . . ."*

But it's time to get breakfast. Lee has gone over to the other side of the island to see whether a certain eagle is golden or only bald, and I've been scribbling, far too long.

Lee will expect flapjacks when he gets back. I'm an expert flapjack-maker by now, for our bread is all gone. Lee is better at the actual flap, however, for when I do it, the flapjack, instead of turning the customary mild summersault, soars so high that it is quite cold by the time it comes down.

I cook fish very well now; my boiled beans with bacon and my outdoor coffee are delicious. The only things I cannot cook are the dried peas. I have boiled some for three days, carrying them hope-fully along with us, setting them on a fire the minute we stop, and still they rattle

stubbornly when the water bubbles. I mean to give them to this chipmunk who thinks he helps me cook. He is the smallest one I have ever seen, and the most engaging. And I'm afraid he knows very well that he is, for he poses outrageously. Now he is sitting on the very tip of a dead cedar bough, eating a prune seed, and only glancing at me fleetingly over his minute shoulder. Sublimely preoccupied!

48

We were marooned yesterday on a sand beach. We went to see some more painted rocks, even more interesting than the first cliff, with moose and men in war canoes and the prints of many hands, all in bright red.

These paintings make the primitive red man seem startlingly alive, much more so than seeing modern Indian culture ever has. Especially these prints of hands. Real hands . . . I had a ghostly feeling.

While Lee was trying to photograph the paintings the wind had streamed down against us harder and harder. White plumes filled the lake till Lee thought it was hazardous to attempt to passage back to the island.

So we scurried on, around a more or less sheltered shore, and found a short sand beach between two vertical cliffs. It was a mere dune between the lake and a swamp beyond, but we took refuge there.

Climbing up ponderable rocks of gray and green and orange to a small cave garlanded with vines, we ate a lunch of cheese and chocolate, which Lee happened to have, luckily, in his pocket. Below us the waves pounded against the sand.

Now, as we sat in our cave, sheltered from the strong gusts, a whole family of moose birds gathered around us, looking at us with friendly eyes, cocking their black-capped heads inquisitively.

This fluffy gray bird is a jay, the Canada jay, also called the camp robber and Whisky Jack, the last derived from his Indian name, Wis-ka-tjon. He seems to have no fear of man at all, though he chooses to live in the wild woods instead of around settlements. I had been wanting to see a moose bird, having heard so many tales of his brazenness and robberies.

But I decided today that he is misjudged.

Crows are crafty and clever thieves, taking an ironic pride in their knavery. But the moose bird is so wide-eyed and innocent — I can't believe he thinks he is a robber at all; he just borrows things, feeling sure you won't mind, since he is a friend of yours.

49

These particular birds sat near us companionably. After a little, Lee set out a crumb of cheese and a crumb of chocolate on the rim of the ledge. Both were snatched up at once. Before long the family was diving and dipping past us, catching slivers of chocolate or cheese or silver paper from our fingers, and perching along the vines. We enjoyed this entertaining in a cave!

After our refreshments had vanished, our guests did too, and we climbed down and explored the hill east of the swamp, till a red squirrel, singing a real little melody up in a tree, saw us and began to scold instead. Really, the animals are as stern with us as they were with Alice in Wonderland. We ruefully made our way back to the beach.

I sat down on the sand and thought delightedly of being reprimanded by a squirrel. I began to realize that one of the deepest joys of this vacation, which I had scarcely been conscious of, is the nature of our social

contacts. So clear, so direct — a squirrel's dislike, the wordless friendship with the jays, the comedy offered by two ants with a flag of dried beef, the awe an ancient pine awakes. After the complicated stresses and emotions a metropolitan day engenders, gatherings where intricate attractions and repulsions web the air, confidences given, advices asked for unsolvable problems, faces in the subway with expressions that tear one's heart . . . Of course one wouldn't want to escape the complex demands forever. But for a breathing space — what a release!

While Lee began a color sketch of the cliff, I lay in the half-shade of tall grass, by a twisted ash tree. When I pillowed my head on my arm I could look along the honey-colored pebbles into a medley of wild-rose briars. Swept by the strong south wind, lulled by the assault of the waves against the sand, I remembered drowsily the first time I ever discovered that poetry had the power to give me cold tingles up and down my back. I could hear the golden voice of our tall young English teacher as clearly as I had when I was thirteen:

> *"And answer made the bold Sir Bedivere:*
> *I heard the ripple washing in the reeds,*
> *And the wild water lapping on the crag. . . .*
>
> *I heard the water lapping on the crag,*
> *And the long ripple washing in the reeds."*

With that murmur in my mind I drifted off to sleep.

When I woke, the wind was more boisterous than ever, and the waves were storming in, so I went wading down the shore. Of course I got drenched, but it didn't matter; I simply went in swimming. It was glorious! The lake glittered darkly blue, the pines were emerald sequins flashing in the wind. Long tangles of water grass wavered in gold-brown streamers about me, and then the brilliant sand shone clear again through the surge. The waves, rough as half-grown puppies, played about me, tossing me over, pushing me back to land.

52

At sunset the wind lessened, and we came back to our island camp.

By the way, Lac la Croix seems to have a reputation for marooning travelers. I have a note from Hugh Faries' diary:

Friday, August 17, 1804

"Embarked this morning and proceeded down to Lake Lacroix, but it blew such a strong head wind, that we did not go far forward. . . . Strong wind and clear weather. [Just like today.]"

Saturday, August 18

"Early this morning we proceeded to the little portage La croix tho' it blew very hard a head. at 1 oclock the men went down with a demie charge to the Pines. they return'd at Sunset having damaged their canoes."

Sunday, September 4th

We decided to come exploring down the Bear Trap River. It is the most unfrequented place that Lee can think of, near by, and he hopes we may find moose. Deer we have seen often, though I've only mentioned one — I *can't* seem to get everything in — but all these days and not one moose has appeared. Lee is quite desperate.

53

The forests were more patrician than usual this morning. Narrow gold diagonals fell through the green-towered ramparts, and the air was cool and touched with fragrance. The water rippled clearly, darkly; outside a shadowy cove the sky to the west bloomed with pale clouds of lavender and faint purple and that creamy fire opals have. I needed some ritual to follow, an orison of worship.

Today we saw our first bear! Lee made me jump by laughing suddenly; he saw it slip from the bluff it was climbing. It fell into the water with a splash, surprising itself and Lee enormously. I was only in time to see a dark shape scramble up the bank, and later, by paddling hard, we had a glimpse of its grotesque silhouette against the skyline for a moment. Lee said that bears will not condescend to hurry if they know you are watching them, but they make up for it as soon as they think they're out of sight.

Later in the morning a gale came up again while we were crossing Iron Lake. The water turned a deep violet, the waves were urgent and white capped. We had to struggle violently to make headway; it was fun, but it was a real combat. Cloud shadows and flashes of sun whirled by us, as we dug our paddles furiously into the surging assault.

"I'll quarter against the wind," Lee shouted to me. "If I drive straight into it, the waves are too close together. We hit too hard."

I was completely exhausted by the time we finally rounded a rugged point and came to smooth, washed shores of pale ivory that were banked by sooty jack pines in close thickets. Here we discovered the mouth of Bear Trap River.

This was a hidden river of abrupt turns and many boulders; remote and casual, it may not have been traversed for many years. A weight of sun lay on its low shores; reeds and rushes and yellow pond lilies, black ducks, blue herons, and bluer kingfishers bedecked it lavishly.

We had lost the wind. It was midsummer and midnoon. We made our way slowly up the river, until we came to a portage. Here was simply

54

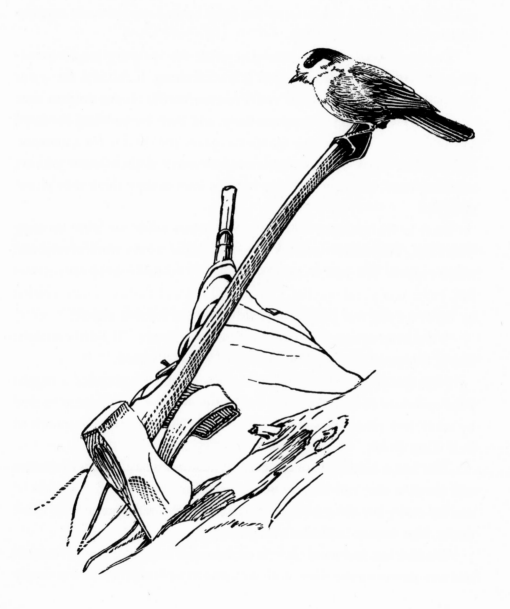

an immense face of cliff, seemingly unscalable, blocking the river, which disappeared in an offhand manner.

Even if it hadn't been remorselessly hot, I was sleepy from fighting the waves all morning. I assembled a modest lunch, though untying the strings of the bag seemed an impossible task. "Hurray," I said to myself, as I gazed at the cliff, "that's stopped us. I can have a nap."

But Lee, fascinated beyond words by the disappearance of the river, was enthusiastic about climbing over the cliff to see what we'd find.

I loathed the idea! I felt fuzzy in my knees, my face was a scarlet flare, and I knew I could never drag myself over the half-mile portage the map promised.

Before I could summon energy to express my violent disapproval, Lee was scrambling up the sheer rock with the canoe balanced on his head; so rebelliously I scrambled too.

We reached the top breathless, and I was allowed to lead the way along a lost path in dense forest. Outwardly a guide, but inwardly a whole mutiny. I hated this path as vehemently as I had loved all our other portages.

Nobody had come here for a long time, we could tell. But there were moose and bear tracks, and I had to scrabble through low branches and tangled places, where I couldn't see what I was going to meet.

I kept stumbling and stubbing my toes. I don't know why I always stub my toes when I am cross; it's one of the minor mysteries of life.

We crossed the portage at last and met the river again. It went placidly on, with grass bogs on either side — a perfect place for moose, Lee was sure. The sun was too hot for me even to mention what I knew perfectly well: there wouldn't be any moose.

There weren't any moose. Nothing alive appeared on that river, except a very drowsy turtle on a rock.

We toiled on down the river, until we came to a place where beavers had been gnawing down trees with industrious teeth and building a super-

solid dam. Even to contemplate the enormous amount of labor they had lavished on it made me feel shattered. Infuriating, haggard, short-winded beasts beavers must be, I thought, working like that. They'd be proud of themselves, too, for being all worn out. I disliked them heartily. But at least their dam stopped our expedition.

When we had dragged ourselves back to the luggage and embarked again, Lee was not long in finding a place to camp. He indicated a rocky point.

"Splendid to watch for moose here."

But I felt supremely indifferent to moose, and it was a very small point. The next possible place, a jack pine wood, I refused too; it was too closely overgrown. The third discovery was a bare rock slope with a little thicket, and black forest beyond.

"There!" said Lee triumphantly.

"It isn't an island," I murmured.

"Of course it is. See that marsh—it probably leads around to the river again." He looked so hot, poor lamb, that I couldn't insist on more paddling. I accepted the place as a possible island, and we landed here.

Lee made me lie down in the shade of a scraggy pine, while he made camp. I was almost asleep when he came gaily along, to show me that a bear had been overturning rocks in search of ants, just by our tent. Like Queen Victoria, I was *not* amused. What if it comes back for an ant it has overlooked?

This really is a magnificent view, with the river curving widely on one side, and a great grass marsh on the other. But it's aloof and alien to me; this isn't an intimate place. I'm not a part of it as I've been in our other camps. I don't want to stay here longer than one night.

September 5th

Today has been superb! Such sudden changes! And we've had a Noah's Ark of animals all day long.

59

It started badly. When we woke it was still hot and sultry, with a heavy feeling in the air. Forest-fire weather, Lee said, and we had breakfast down by the water, to be especially careful. A dismal breakfast in the sun, with the flapjacks gummy, cold coffee, and no fruit. For I'd forgotten to stew any of the dried fruits and bears have eaten the blueberries from this slope. Also, I spilled the prepared milk. And I felt disgruntled because the management had furnished no sand to scour my skillet, nor any soft thick grass to clear the dishes with.

Never mind. We went off to investigate the eastern swamp, which had an evasive fascination. Rivulets filtered through the slipping grass. Strange plants swayed in the shadowy greenness under our paddles. Little three-petaled flowers, frail as apple blossoms, floated awry in the swamp pools, where tenuous shapes wavered and dissolved. It was a sliding place, without validity.

But a west wind came up, and the air lightened. We found a small stream which led us to a hidden pond. Peering through the ice-green poplars, we discovered six deer bathing in the water! Like nymphs they looked, careless and unafraid. We watched them with delight until a splendid buck suddenly appeared on the far shore. Just for a glancing moment; then he caught our scent, and so we lost them all.

We started back in high spirits, with a kingfisher darting like a blue arrow ahead of us. Then I heard a noise. Like something crying.

"Lee, what is it?"

He listened. "It might be a bear cub."

It was a porcupine, up in a cedar tree, with its head between its paws, crying and crying.

One couldn't comfort a porcupine, but I got out on the bank to see it, and caught sight of another one, climbing a tall poplar. Hand over hand he went, like a man, and then swung hilariously on a high branch in the wind.

As we came back toward camp, Lee saw still another, walking around

60

our tent, the rascal. We were deluged with porcupines. When we reached the tent, we chased the intruder up a tree, and Lee threw my hat at him.

"Why, Lee!" I cried.

However, when I rescued the hat, it was skewered with several of the quills, which come out so easily whenever anything brushes against a  porcupine, and so I could examine the needle point and the myriad barbs along each quill.

The fourth creature appeared down among the lily pads, swimming absurdly with both paws at once. I'd never heard of porcupines in the water, and I didn't expect it of them. Porcupines are so *dry* — it's like seeing a cactus take to swimming. But it seems the quills are slim tubes of air and buoy them up like water wings.

All afternoon was swift with clouds. The wind grew damp with coming rain, while a menace of navy blue piled up in the west.

Lee decided he saw a deer at the end of the bay, and if we slipped down along the grassy bank we would be quite close to her. She was looking so intently across the inlet that she didn't see us until we were within a canoe's length. Then off she went in a tremendous bound.

Then we saw why she had been gazing so steadily. Her spotted fawn had balked on the other bank. It looked at us with great soft eyes. We knew each other intimately, for one moment, before it disappeared.

As we came out into Bear Trap River again, it began to rain. At the same moment, "Moose!" Lee exclaimed.

I caught a glimpse of something brown downstream. Then it disappeared behind an outcrop of rock. What did rain matter when we could realize our ambition at last? We tore downstream. There it was. A cow moose in the water.

62

I stopped paddling; I was too excited not to splash. Then suddenly, beyond her we caught sight of a bull moose!

Two great prehistoric creatures in front of us, like the monsters you see in dreams.

We came closer and closer to them. Till I thought we were quite close enough, and began to talk. Loud enough to be noticed, I hoped.

For moose think very slowly, and they might have been muddle-headed enough to make a wrong turn and plunge into the canoe instead of away from it, if they were very suddenly surprised. Lee is almost too expert at creeping up on creatures.

When they finally did see us, they didn't believe in us. They gazed incredulously as we edged nearer. Then at last they splashed madly through the shallows away from us. Up the bank they went, breaking into the rocking trot I had been afraid I'd never see, and then we caught a last glimpse of them against the hill, between yellowing poplars.

We went home in triumph. Through a thunderstorm and a sunset, both at once, a sight most weirdly glorious.

A wild magenta light on the hills, the river in deep purple shadow, a blaze of flame color lighting the thunderheads above us, while jagged lightning, electric blue, zigzagged everywhere. It was like the Doré pictures in our *Paradise Lost*.

Especially when two fallen angels came coasting down the wind into the swamp. This was almost too much! When they settled down and transformed themselves into great blue herons, I felt greatly relieved.

Tuesday, September 6th

Of course it had to be last night, just after I had seen what mammoth creatures moose are! One came along in the middle of the night, took fright at our tent, and pounded off through the woods like a runaway locomotive. Such crashes from an Oriniack! I'm quite sure now I'd rather see than hear one.

64

I lay awake a long while, looking out at the dark, feeling that over-mastering awe of the black night and its terrors which is our inheritance from savage ancestors.

But I want the alarums as well as the excursions; I wouldn't want to miss the discords of these wild fastnesses.

We broke camp early this morning and fished on our way down the river, which was held captive in nets of white fog. I caught three bass, and we watched a mink wander along the shore, like a country gentleman out for a stroll.

We came out into the wide lake again. There was never a morning so completely flawless. Sky-blue water, wide shores backed by the dim lilac of pine ranges, great cloud foams of white and lavender piled up far behind them. Yet shore and clouds, great as they were, only a narrow strip between the pure blue above and below. When these big lakes are still—do you remember, when you were small, they filled a glass of water full for you, and then put on one more drop, so that the water stood up over the edge of the glass? These lakes seem overfull of beauty, like that, and sometimes I can hardly bear it.

September 7th

This is, I think, the most perfect camp of all. How can I say that, when they are all so different? When our three sapphire lakes were so especially glamorous? But that was a misted fairytale place. This is a clear carved design—true poetry.

It is so savagely sweet here; a pagan loveliness—Grecian paganism, untouched and pure. With all its wildness you would never be afraid.

Yesterday we meant to explore the bays on Lac la Croix. But on a small wild-rice bay there was a tantalizing portage to Lake McAree, and we found ourselves over here.

In the afternoon, I saw an Elysian island ahead of us and begged for it. There seemed no place to land, but it looked so mysteriously perfect

66

we went all around it, and found at last a secluded horseshoe to the north, where we could push in between fallen trees and water plants.

This island seemed never to have had anyone set foot on it. A most ancient and primeval place, all deep shadows and thick green moss and queer tall boulders. No wide sunny spaces, only bits of gold. Dark hollows filled with densely matted pine needles and vine tangles, doubled twisted trees leaning low over the water. There was no place to camp at all. But we felt held here, like Rat and Mole from *The Wind in the Willows;* we expected to hear the mighty Piper at any moment.

A little farther on we found a sunnier island, and another darker one, with a small and shimmering bay between. As we came into it, six mallard ducks were swimming there. They flew up as we came close, and went skimming around us and off over the trees.

As we went on, a single duck, flying up from the woods, went south and then came circling back. This was the mother duck, Lee was sure, and her children had already disappeared.

On through a narrow channel with a clean pine wood on the east shore, and around the corner we found a lily pond, peaceful and silvered; then we went past a point to a wide blue lake again. We didn't need to see any more. We came back through the inlet, and after hesitating between the clear pine wood and the sunlit island, we somehow chose the island.

When we landed, the great pine trunks were gilded with light, and ferns and mats of blueberries were enameled mosaics, gold, green-gold, and green-blue. There was a breath of scented wind, and then we heard a hermit thrush singing, the first one we have heard in our canoe country. That most haunting gold-dark song, golden with realized rapture, dark with unrealized grief — I shall never hear it again without longing for this place.

Lee made our camp above a ledge of rocks, in the midst of treetops. It was the hottest middle of the afternoon and I lay on my back in gray moss, soft and thick, in the shadow of the widest pine, and began a poem,

When the blue light comes
Through the great pine wood,
Clear and unblown
As blue light should —

while Lee chopped down trees with reckless enjoyment, and the mother duck flew wildly over the island, calling for her children.

When it was cooler and long shadows flung themselves down the hill, I cooked supper, while Lee cleaned the fish I had caught on the way down. I picked blueberries by the bush; it's quicker that way, and they make an exotic centerpiece, with the luminous berries, exquisite as flowers, and the pointed leaves now turned to crimson lacquer.

I had my most attractive place for camp cooking. A crack down the rocks for my fireplace, the flat top of the stony ledge for my table, and glimpses through interlaced boughs, over islands and golden water. Lee chopped a path down through the ash trees to the east shore, a little vista through green leaves, down to green ripples and slim reeds.

I was so enchanted with our home that I made a blueberry shortcake for supper, the first baking I've tried, using sweetened biscuit dough for the cake and the largest of my covered pots for an oven. It was a flagrant triumph.

As we ate supper we could see the blue night coming up the eastern sky. Blue night over there, and it was approaching us, step by step. I had never seen it come so unmistakably. It grew darker, and the small moon brightened. The shores and islands became black blots, and the moon began to make a faint rainbow path on the lake.

This half-moon made everything around us more solitary. I suppose because I've watched just such a moon so often at home. The island felt *farther away* than any place I've ever been.

Lee and I sat on the cliff's edge. Our duck came swimming around the island, from moonlight to dark shadow, still calling her lost children. She was so small a figure in the night, and she wasn't calling frantically now, but in a subdued way, reassuringly and tenderly.

When at last the mosquitoes drove us into our tent, there was still a view, through the netting, of black branches and a great emerald star.

Wild clouds, too, that grew wilder and heavier, till a terrific storm broke in the west. The lightning and thunder became almost continuous and the wind whooped in the trees. Lee got really worried about the tent's blowing away.

"Shall we pack everything?" he said. "Though if the tent goes it will be so tragic that all the little things might as well blow away too!"

We grew more and more hilarious as the wind blew harder and harder, and I laughed so at Lee's trying to hold on to three corners of the tent at once, dashing around like one of our chipmunks, that I could hardly hold the one corner I was responsible for.

We even made up songs about the tent, hoping it would be flattered enough to stay with us, and from that we progressed to all the old songs we'd ever known. It must have been surprising to the owls to hear

> *"Steamboat Bill, steaming down the Mississippi,*
> *Tryin' to break the record of the Robert E. Lee!"*

coming from an unsteady small tent, rocking on a rockbound shore, in the middle of a thunderstorm and the middle of the night.

September 9th

Ten days now since we've seen any human beings. It's quite a record. I haven't missed them at all.

This morning was washday. Down the path Lee had cleared, I carried my laundry to the jade-green pool shielded by lemon-scented bushes. Blackberry vines curled near. Some delicate dry grasses of pale cream

71

stood against the brilliant water. I splashed and rubbed my clothes on the stones and felt very archaic.

Spreading my array on the bushes to dry, I retreated to the pine shade. Here the moss was soft and brightly green, and I lay full length in it. So I discovered its flowers.

Flowers of the moss. I'd like to make a diminutive study of them. Shallow cups of pale green, bright scarlet tips enameled on green stems, tarnished silver discs. Coral dots, tawny seed pods high on slender threads, brown-petaled cups, gold points, rose points, gray-green trumpets. There is a deep gray moss like masses of tiny shrubs, a green velvet that covers stones as smoothly as upholstery, a pale green lichen like minute oak leaves. All these atoms are so *sturdy* in their miniature loveliness. I want to keep them.

This afternoon we came over to the ancient island. I am drifting around in the canoe, while Lee has gone ashore to sketch.

I'm in the bottom of the canoe, lying back against our coats. It's very still. Just a little lapping of the water on the stone near me — that's the only sound. Now and then I can hear Lee crashing somewhere on the island.

Such deep gloom up through the trees! Down here there are water plants whose graceful curled leaves start deep in the brown water, and reeds whose slender jointed stems sway high above the flat lily pads. Long swaths of grass lie on the liquid surface in irregular circles. Over the water a Norway pine swoops down; its lovely horizontal branches, its blue-green needles and rough twigs are reflected sharply. There are tiny warblers flying all through it, like truant piano notes. I'm so happy I can almost fly too.

We have been down to the rapids fishing. I laughed till I cried down there; any whoops the loons made were nothing to mine. As I stepped out of the canoe the rock was slippery and my foot slid into the water. Lee has been training me, ever since we started, in the proper way to enter

72

and leave a canoe, so now he said reprovingly, "No sense in that!" Then *he* stepped steadily out, on the same treacherous stone, and went, *zipp*, down on his back in the lake. I never saw such an amazed expression. "No sense in that, Lee!" I said sternly.

September 10th

The sunset yesterday was Blake's "eternity in an hour." Great bubbles of clouds, cream and soft fire and amethyst, floating over all the world, in a sky so boundless that the world was only a small, dimmer bubble itself. When I lay back against the rocks, and looked up into the intense soft blue, with great circles of pink and rose and soft lilac gleaming there, I was transformed from an earth creature into an airy one.

Feeling so light in spirit, I went canoeing. Lee remained lazily on shore, but I set out alone without a qualm. Only, when I got out into the lake and gusts of wind assailed me, I realized suddenly that it had been absolutely calm on the former occasions when I had been sole navigator. And then I had had a load to steady the canoe. Now it was empty-headed and as hard to control as most empty-headed people are. Its bow rose defiantly in the air. I couldn't manage to keep any direction. I bobbed around like a circus horse.

Lee began to shout from the shore, but his advice was mostly blown away. I felt as frantic as I do when I'm talking excitedly over the telephone and the family keeps calling additions and contradictions from the next room! In trying to follow the remnants of counsel which came to me, and to control my canoe and my laughter, I somehow got a violent cramp in my right hand.

Now I did curvet wildly! I couldn't get the bow headed toward the island; the wind spun me back every time. I was amazed at the canoe, usually so obedient to Lee's slightest gesture; it was up in arms against me. With no authority at all, I went drifting down the lake to an unknown destination.

I began to have misgivings. What *was* going to happen to me? It looked as if I might blow across the lake.

If I did that, I'd have to wait on the far shore till the wind went down. Probably I'd be there all night. I had no matches with me for a fire — not even a coat for a cover. And Lee would be frightened about me. For that matter I'd be horribly frightened about myself. In the mornings we always found footprints of things that had walked along the shores in the night. I didn't want to stay on a dark shore and meet them. But I'd never dare go back into the forest depths —

I looked despairingly back at Lee, safe on our cliff.

He was just giving me up as hopeless. Resignedly, as I watched, he sat down and began to unlace his boots.

The next thing I knew he was swimming to the mainland, and then he came dashing along the rocks, parallel to my course. But I was in the lee of the island now, and sheltered from the wind; so by peculiar paddling I managed to approach the shore. Lee waded out and boarded the craft, and I was ignominiously wafted homeward.

I began to wish I hadn't laughed so unrestrainedly at Lee in the afternoon. It had set a bad example.

"No sense in this, my dear! No sense in this! — And if it hadn't been for that spot of calm I suppose I'd be galloping for miles around all those deep bays, to keep you from going down the rapids at the end of the lake!"

But in spite of his hilarity I found myself hoping that he would *not* break his strong right arm, or even his left one. In fact I hoped fervently that nothing at all would happen to him. For it was evident that if anything did, it would take me years to get us back to Winton.

I awoke in the middle of the night to feel deeply thankful that I was safe on our island and not stranded on some solitary shore. I got up and slipped out of the tent to see what midnight was really like. Under an ink-black pine, looking out over the dim water, I felt strange and small.

The wind had died. The stillness had an inexplicable poignancy. Those immensities of land and water — they belonged to porcupines walking in the moonlight, to slender deer, and heavy shuffling bears.

I tried to picture this region in midwinter. The flawless white. Snowy hills, snowy pines with glints of hidden jade, vast levels of snowy lake. A drifted purity broken only by track patterns, from the tiny footprints of the wood mice to the great crashes of the moose. The frosted vapor coming up from the rapids, encrusting the branches with silver, drifting down the shores like the ghosts of the caribou that used to wander here. Deer standing on their hind legs to eat the cedars, a pileated woodpecker shocking the snowy silence with his scarlet and white and black. Timber wolves trotting along the ice, skirting the shores —

And at that I heard a wolf howl, far down the lake. Again the howl came, unmistakable. After the blood-curdling moose call, this seemed only pleasantly eerie, especially as it was a distant sound. Still, I went inside the tent again.

This afternoon we went over to the lily pond to read *The King's Henchman*. White water lilies lay on the black water; white birches, delicate poplars, and dark cedars were mingled on three sides. On the fourth was a gigantic hill, with straight Norway pines towering up magnificently between moss-deep rocks. Their strength was a powerful contrast to all the lacelike beauty near by.

We climbed into the branches of a pine which hung far out over the water, and dangled our feet and read Millay to our hearts' content. Then we swam in the ebony pool—so different from our usual sunny beaches—and tried picking water lilies under water.

Tomorrow we start retracing our path, so I suppose my notebook will end here. I've just noticed that I never seem to write down the last few days in any of our journeys. Probably because when my thoughts begin to turn with joy toward home, I don't want to realize the fact of departure. Probably, too, I am not as deep in the moment's adventure. Not that there is less enjoyment in these hours, but we are already changing from the present to the future tense. And then I never like to say good-by.

Lee is hurrying now to finish his sketch of the deep forest, before the light fails. It is his last chance, for we are starting out at dawn tomorrow morning.

It is time for us to go. The food pack is very light to lift. There is a look of autumn in the sunlight now, though no frosty air has touched us. The blueberry leaves have been crimson ever since we've been here, but now the stray birches are shining yellow among the dark pines down the shore.

Yet we do not need to hurry too fast on our way back, for we have five days left before we must reach Winton. We mean to take practically the same paths and portages. The leaves along the stony hills will be flaming gold and scarlet soon—we are looking forward to that.

But I don't want to leave. I'll always remember this place and long for it a little. Islands of gold and green, the wind in great branches, an owl's call in the rainy dusk, the scent of our wood smoke drifting across the moonlight. It will be like a lost kingdom.

78

ACKNOWLEDGMENTS

In so informal and personal a book as this, a conventional preface in the usual place might have come between the reader and the good companions who were sharing their experience with him. But now that the journey is ended, and the spell broken, we can thank those who made it possible.

First, of course, Mrs. Jaques, who graciously consented to expand into a book sketches contributed to the *American Girl* and to the *Portal*. To the discerning editors of these magazines we make grateful acknowledgment of the permission to reprint those parts of the book which appeared in their pages.

And equally Mr. Jaques, for complementing his wife's sensitivity and gaiety with his knowledge of the wilderness and with the sure vigor and beauty of his drawing. Mr. Jaques' bird habitat groups in the American Museum of Natural History are the delight of thousands. His paintings illustrate *Florida Bird Life, The Birds of Minnesota*, and *Oceanic Birds of South America;* he has done black and white sketches for many of the books by Dr. Frank M. Chapman. Some of the drawings in this book are adapted from illustrations for an article in *Natural History*. We thank its editors for permission to use them in this way.

The Publishers